AF443840

Remnant Halos - The Angel's Guardians Prequel

Want to know the story about Director Emilio and his life-time lover? Get the prequel to this series for FREE. Click on the link now to download: https://dl.bookfunnel.com/ovzzd2h3t1

I must return to Heaven, even if it will break my heart.

As an angel, I have no business getting tangled up with Creatures on Earth, especially vampires. But when vampire

Emilio's attempt to rescue innocent witches ends up in his own death, I can't simply watch on. Even though I know the punishment, I bring him back to life, and thus, fall from Heaven.

Soon, my white-hair, huge wings, and angelic powers attract unwanted attention. I must return to Heaven. If I stay, I'll end up as a prized prey of human hunters who will stop at nothing to claim my angelic powers for themselves.

Together with Emilio, I start my journey to the tallest point of the land, the gateway to Heaven. As we avoid my pursuers, I can't help but fall for reckless, kind, and funny Emilio. He might be a Creature of darkness, but he's perfect for me.

Yet with each day I spend on Earth, I grow weaker, and my chances of reaching Heaven dwindle. Even if I make it to the top of the mountain, I'll have to face the hardest choice ever. Because if I'm permitted to return to heaven, I'll never see Emilio again.

Remnant Halos is the prequel to The Angel's Guardians series. Don't miss this delicious paranormal romance read filled with magic, forbidden love, and heart-pounding action!

Download now for FREE: https://dl. bookfunnel.com/ovzzd2h3t1

DEMONIC AFFAIRS

A REVERSE HAREM PARANORMAL FANTASY (ANGEL'S GUARDIANS BOOK 2)

CALLIE STONE

PARIS IN THE SUMMERTIME

Natasha

"Garçon!"

As Alexander summoned the waiter over for another Café Americain, I could not help a soft little sigh to myself.

It was not a loud sigh, like the huff of total annoyance which Michael let out, nor was it even audible. It was a wistful, tingly little shiver which I was feeling all too often since my team set up shop in France.

It was the feeling of being irritated, and charmed, and amused, and frustrated with the feelings which had only continued to grow since our arrival—feelings I suspected would only become worse over time.

"Oh, for crying out loud, man!" I knew Michael would have to punctuate his own sigh with a verbal jab at our vampire teammate. "Everybody here speaks English. And on top of that, everybody knows what that word, garçon, means, so it's not even impressive."

"Of course, we all do," huffed Kieran, confused in a way

that was far more endearing than it was irritating. "We always speak English, what are you even talking about?"

"I mean, all the Parisians speak English," Michael interrupted, letting out another one of his typical Michael-sighs. This one, like many of his other exasperated little exhales, was delightfully tinged with savage drollness.

"And they're all French," argued Alexander, with a typically clear-cut point.

"Well, yes…but still…"

"So, what does Garçon mean?" challenged Alexander.

"It means fuck you, you vampire fuck." Michael grinned, and I held back a chuckle myself as the waiter brought Alexander another glass of water—which just like his coffee would sit untouched.

"Geez! That's not at all what it means!" Kieran protested. He was taking it all much too seriously, but doing his best to keep the peace. "It means boy!"

I just enjoyed what was becoming my standard social role in my team—laughing—before the sound of the café doors opening cued us to glance over to see who had entered.

We were all trying to subtly observe the comings and goings of the popular spot, surreptitiously glancing over was becoming something of an art for all of us.

Strolling in from the boulevard with absurd poise were two exceptionally, nigh curiously attractive women. They were graceful, lithe, dressed from head to toe in Chanel and Dior——it was as if they'd just stepped in from a damn catalogue. One was short with ginger hair, and hid behind huge sunglasses; the other was the classic tall, blonde archetype.

"Well," remarked Kieran in a hushed tone, "she's one to pay attention to for sure."

It was a curious statement, especially as we had so little experience trying to spot creatures out in the wild at that point in such a public-facing way. I had to wonder what

Kieran meant. Did he identify her as a werewolf such as himself? Or a sprite, or a vampire?

Looking her over myself, then looking back at the slight flush on Kieran's cheeks, I realised that she was none of the above.

"Very funny," I sighed, causing Kieran to adorably blush a deeper shade of red.

It is certainly not like any of us were very comfortable out in the open in the world of humans.

At least I wasn't.

Especially this new practice of acting so comfortable sitting out in the open in the midst of a popular café in a capital city as if it were bloody nothing.

Yet Kieran, whose tortured past amongst his werewolf brood could have, by all rights, lost him as weary of humanity as any of us, was apparently testing the waters of feeling right at home checking out the French ladies in a Parisian bloody coffee shop.

Or maybe Kieran was just trying to get me to chuckle a bit.

It was awkward, yet, as per usual with Kieran's ventures out of his shell to show a teasing fondness, oddly flattering.

Plus, by that point, it would have been fair to say that it seemed as though neither the ginger lady nor her lanky blonde friend were of any interest for our purposes. My teammates had lost interest and gone back to looking into their empty wine glasses and mugs.

Alexander's gaze kept flitting over to a table at the far corner of the café, where an attractive couple in their late twenties were arguing in French. Most of the café was naturally trying to ignore their raised voices, but Alexander seemed to be subtly observing them.

"What's up?" I asked.

"Them," he said. "The man and woman arguing."

Pretending to stretch, I slowly spread my arms out and let

out a dramatic yawn capped off with a little puppyish squeak, craned my neck over to one side and then the other, giving me a closer look at the couple.

They looked like a generic, nearly nondescript young married couple. Yet I knew that Alexander could recognise his own kind, at least as well as any of us.

"Well?" I asked.

"Do you think we should try to approach him?" Alexander raised an eyebrow at me. "There's something there."

It was notable that Alexander had used the term 'approach' rather than 'recruit'. Our methods had been changing, or at least some of the newer approaches we'd been debating were novel to the degree that much of it felt new. At that point in our stint in Paris we were basically on reconnaissance and even approaching seemed like a risky proposition.

Heck, even if I were a vampire, I would not be thrilled about approaching a vampire in such an environment.

Alexander seemed to find it worthwhile to seek my opinion, so I gave it some thought.

We had substantial direction from Director Hask as to how to go about recruitment in the delicate atmosphere of the City of Lights, but then we'd spent the entire rental car ride from London to Paris arguing our own opinions on it. As far as I was concerned, we were in a safe place for Alexander to attempt approaching a fellow vampire.

"Maybe," I replied at last to Alexander's question. Not as committal as he may have liked, but he had to appreciate how I'd deliberated.

There had been an uptick of reports of creatures in central Paris and throughout the city as of late, and our little social hangs at the café near our flat were ostensibly to stake out one popular spot for such sightings.

There was reason to be cautious, but we all felt an obligation to help those such as ourselves who found danger in the human world.

I rolled my eyes as the couple began to bicker again—partially in annoyance at my own inability to understand what they were saying—especially as their voices grew louder.

I knew that immersion would help bring my Français skills to fluency in an acceptably short period of time, yet I was growing impatient—and frankly a bit embarrassed—at my own lack of French cogency, especially compared to some of the boys' command of the tongue.

Especially Troy's. In spite of perpetually keeping the pointy tips of his fae ears hidden underneath the type of ball cap you'd expect to see on an American tourist, his underlying regal classiness came out the moment a word of perfectly pronounced French left his lips.

But at that time, Troy and the whole team, along with a growing number of the other café patrons, were silent as the couple's verbal sparring rose to increasingly embarrassing volumes.

After a few moments the yelling suddenly, eerily stopped. In the relative quiet that followed, I could hear the couple speaking in hushed, apologetic tones to each other.

I looked back at them in the corner of the café, and they were now holding hands. They looked happy together, abruptly, though the man had a distant look in his eyes.

I held out my hand for Alexander to give me my glass of wine, which he did with a smirk.

"I do drink wine." My joke, a reference to the original Bela Lugosi Dracula film, was meant as a witty comment like we all made frequently. Yet it came out much flirtier than I'd intended.

Luckily, my comment was thoroughly ignored by all.

"Alright," I said, intending to try for a do-over. "I'll take that glass of wine for ya."

"Makes no sense." Alexander smirked before standing up to stride over to where the couple were sitting.

I took a big gulp of merlot.

"You really think that he should just waltz over there?" Kieran asked in that earnest way of his.

"Let's watch and see," I replied softly.

All eyes were on Alexander—at least mine were—as he approached the couple. I could see the man flashing his teeth at him, just enough for a tiny glimpse for Alexander to get the message from one vampire to another:

Yes, I'm like you, and I don't know why you're bothering me, but it can't be good so buzz off!

Although I couldn't hear their conversation, I could see the woman looking up at Alexander with an expression of subtle terror, clutching onto her boyfriend's arm.

My next instinct was to take a quick glance around the café. It seemed as though no one had noticed. The man knew that Alexander was a vampire, though, and had signalled to him to stay far away.

I heard some mumbling from the corner of the room and saw that it was the café manager who was on his phone. I strained my ears, and was just able to make out what he was saying in fluent French.

"Je ne sais pas ce qui se passe, mais appelle la police."

That last word—*police*—was obvious if nothing else, and my French was at least to the point where I had gotten the gist regardless.

He knew, or at least suspected, that something bad was about to happen.

"I can't hear. What's he saying?" Kieran asked eagerly, leaning over to me.

"He's saying we need to get out as quickly as we can without attracting attention," Troy muttered. And he was right.

"Well, what are we waiting for?" Kieran said. "Let's go!"

I felt a rush of excitement as the four of us stood together, the type of adrenaline hit I'd not expected that evening.

"That's it!" Troy yelled suddenly, play-acting a scenario to explain our sudden departure. "I've had it up to here with you all." I tried not to laugh. "Let's go, let's go."

"Bye, Alexander," I said sweetly. "It was so nice to see you," I drawled sarcastically.

I was pretty sure I was doing an over-the-top impersonation of a Southern American accent, even though everyone there had heard my usual British accent already. Didn't matter, I was having fun.

"Ciao, Alexander," Michael called out.

"Bye, now," Kieran added in a charmingly, hilariously quiet attempt to join in.

The four of us legged it out of there, passing beautiful art pieces and luxurious furniture on the way out. However, as much as I'd always enjoyed seeing the café's usual décor, an even better, or more relieving sight at that moment was the vampire and his partner making their own way safely out of the building's lesser-known side entrance.

We may have had an expectedly contentious approach with the vampire, but at least he had been able to get out before a potential total disaster.

Alexander threw a bunch of euro notes on the table before following us out. I admired that; he'd screwed up our recruitment attempt, so he paid for our drinks.

"Hurry up!" Alexander hissed, perhaps a bit too loudly and mostly, seemingly, in frustration at himself as he was tailing behind us.

None of us were especially used to working this way.

"You moron!" chided Michael once we'd all made it out onto Boulevard Saint-Marcel, although his apparent anger had already begun to dissolve into more of a lighthearted, mocking tone before he had even finished yelling.

It seemed we had mostly likely avoided a couple of close

calls. While Alexander's track record for that evening was not up to his own typical standards, I think we all understood at that point that some of us were allowed an off night every now and then.

"Shut up!" Alexander interrupted. "We're going back to the flat, now!"

Naturally, all of us had to laugh at him ordering us around as usual, especially with his frequent expounding on the egalitarian nature of our team.

As outsiders in the world of humans, all of us had some sense of trouble afoot. The feeling that we'd made it out of that potential mess without harm was palpable as we made it back to our flat across the Seine.

The flat itself was located in the top level of a beautiful townhouse just off the Boulevard de la Bastille, from where we had a good view of the area around us. It was not a rented flat, but indeed property of the congregation, a pied-a-terre that was meant for such uses.

Unfortunately, the smallish flat was not exactly designed for more than a couple tenants—and certainly wasn't ideal for a team of our size—but as I'd kept telling myself, being put on assignment in central Paris had to come with some sacrifices.

It was only fair.

After we'd climbed the ageing steps and entered the flat, my eyes as usual traveled up to the semi-private loft area set aside for my bed and possessions. It was the nicest 'room' that any of us had in the flat and I tried my best to acknowledge that, at least to myself, when I could.

I kept hoping that habit of gratitude would eventually help subdue some of the frustrations and awkwardness of living there with my lovely yet distracting teammates.

And, as usual, there was an awkward moment of all of us standing under the fluorescent lighting of the common area after walking in.

These moments may have been uncomfortable, but I'd begun to think of them, at least privately, as sort of an 'opening credits' moment, or perhaps a big panel of a comic book, in which you got to see all the main heroes just standing together, being silent yet maybe a bit badass as a team.

Michael the Shapeshifting Trickster!

Kieran the Werewolf!

Alexander the Vampire!

Troy the Fae!

And, your main hero (hey, it's all in my head, after all):

Natasha the sassy and quite fetching Angel!

The fabulous team sent straight from the congregation in London by Director Hask to recruit, save, and even fight for creatures such as themselves trying to survive in the world of humans!

It all seemed quite exciting when I thought about it that way, even when my reality was my teammates starting to mill about and grumble about what the hell they were going to do with the rest for the evening.

You would think that the reality of it would be less exciting. It usually was, with such flights of fancy. Yet, in a way, I was finding myself in a reality as exciting as any daydream I'd ever had.

"Man, I am jonesing for a few quick reps after all that espresso," announced Kieran, pulling his shirt off over his head while heading over to the set of free weights the boys insisted on keeping in the bloody living room.

It was just not the kind of exciting I needed surrounding me at all times, day and night.

"You work out," declared Alexander as he tore off his corduroy jacket, revealing the thin mock turtleneck shirt clinging to his well-toned frame. "But I work," he continued, walking towards the set of research folios and the work laptop set up on the living room coffee table, insisting on walking in a manner which maximised the sculpted beauty of his rock-hard gluteus goddamn maximus as he did so.

It was a most unwelcome sort of distraction indeed, leaving me standing flustered and a bit a-swoon as I could not help but watch in the entryway.

"I need to start roasting the arabica beans so they can properly off-gas before tomorrow's breakfast." Troy had also decided to join in on this trend of the boys announcing declaring their activities out loud, albeit with his standard formality.

At least he is not opting to take his shirt off like the others, I thought.

But the small amount of relief even that thought provided did not last long as Troy strode towards the kitchenette and shed his thin, green jumper, slinging it over his shoulder. I was left staring at the impressive upper back and abdominal muscles which rippled every time he took a step.

I decided to ignore everyone and just go back to my room to have pleasant dreams thinking about the more romanticised version of my life.

"I don't care what you all do," I said blandly, a non-sequitur making little sense to anyone and probably making less sense to myself.

Alone in my room, staring up at the weathered ceiling, I was having trouble sleeping yet again. I couldn't stop thinking about that evening, about all of these distractingly gorgeous boys I'd been teamed up with. Eventually I did fall into slumber, and opening my eyes I found myself in that wonderful place where I'd last seen my mother: the angel Gatriel. "Mum?"

It was as I'd remembered from that last dream: azure skies, rolling fields, a city of gems and gold in the distance. In the fields were animals, not of flesh and blood but of refined light, lazuli hues and viridian shades.

It was like a growing, ever-evolving dreamscape. It

became both more real and richly detailed as well as more majestically surreal and unearthly each time I witnessed it. It was like a parallel reality to my own, becoming at least as real as my own—yet Gatriel remained the exact same wondrous and comforting presence each time my dreams took me there.

"Keep your focus, my angel baby," I heard Gatriel whisper. "You need to wake up now."

"No, I'm not ready!" I heard myself say, although I wasn't sure why. "I have questions. I want to stay here with you."

"Natasha, wake up," I heard my angelic mother say firmly, and suddenly I was back in my bed in the flat, still hearing the words "wake up" echoed through my mind.

"I've been less than angelic," I heard myself sleep-slurring as the dream faded. "My thoughts."

"You're an angel to me always." My mum's voice seemed to echo out of nowhere as I opened my eyes to the empty bedroom.

"I'm not a real angel," I protested automatically, but then I heard something creak in the living room.

I recognised the sounds and aromas of Troy cooking breakfast in the kitchenette just outside my makeshift bedroom. I could smell the heavenly aromas of sautéed onions, olive oil, eggs, and—yes, even for breakfast—red wine. It may have been morning, still, but Troy had a magical way with the stuff I was addicted to, the way he would use it to enhance the flavour profile of nearly everything he made. I put some clothes on and went out to help my teammate—or at the very least, take in the magnificent aroma of what he was preparing.

"Did you just cook?" I enquired. "That's my job!"

It definitely was not my job and it even more definitely was Troy's job, but even after a rather serious dream—or perhaps because of it—I had decided to be in a less than serious mood.

"You were snoozing!" he retorted. "I had to get breakfast ready…I thought it'd be easier than waking you."

"Well, thanks," I replied quietly and a bit ashamed both at my yelling and my failure to convey a teasing tone.

I mean, could he have possibly thought I was *serious*? My complaint would have been absurd on the face of it—is not as if I were doing any cooking compared to Troy or at all for that matter.

But considering that as Troy's brekkie fry-up magic was filling the kitchenette area, I realised I was also blushing—or *really* blushing—for a different reason entirely.

Out of all the boys with whom I shared that tiny flat, and with whom I'd gotten to know so well over during our time together, Troy was likely the only one who would not only assume I was serious with such a complaint, but also very likely the only one of those boys who would bother taking the time to address it seriously as well.

Either that, or he was having a bit of a flirt with me, which was also a reason to blush even if it were not quite *as* touching.

As usual, Troy didn't seem to notice my blushing, regardless of its cause, or much else about me even as he turned some small part of his attention in my direction. Rather, he just kept happily working on his breakfast fry-up, smiling confidently—maybe with a touch of obliviousness—with his eyes fixed down upon the skillet.

I found myself sighing again, this time louder than I would have liked. I wasn't sure of the response I'd expected, but there was something inside me that just needed to scream out:

"Can't you lot all just put your shirts on or something so I can try to keep my head about me in this damn place?"

As I was lost in what was becoming an annoyingly common reverie, Troy had finished whatever he had presently been doing with his culinary wizardry and had at last loosened his gaze on the skillet, choosing at that moment to look over at me instead. Our eyes met, and I felt a sinking feeling in my stomach. Whatever frustration I had about my teammates' and current flatmates' habits—and it was a frustration I was not shy about sharing when it got to be too much—was something I realized I was likely written all over my expression as I glared at poor Troy.

Troy who had been doing nothing but try to cook in the wonderful way he always did.

"What's wrong?" he asked. "Is there something on my face?"

"I'm going shopping." My eyes were turned downward onto the cracked kitchen tile. I could not think of anything better to say, but at that moment I needed to get out, to go somewhere, maybe out of my own slight embarrassment or maybe out of the continuously pent-up frustration of living there or some combination of all the above, but I just wanted, needed to go.

And *shopping* was about the only reason I had to do that.

"I'll go with you," Troy offered. For some reason his offer felt like a massive weight lifting from my spirit.

"Really?" What I had really wanted to ask, instead of that vague, unformed question, was what type of shopping he thought I was doing, because I was not sure yet myself.

But also, did he really want to go with me, or was it just some *Troy* version of being polite?

"May I please take you grocery shopping, my dear?" Troy responded, answering my unspoken question about the kind of shopping, and also sounding sincere enough to mean it beyond mere civility.

Plus, none of my teammates had ever called me *that* before, at least not since we had been in Paris. Honestly, part of me wanted to give Troy what-for for being fresh with me. However, after my eyes finally traveled up to meet with his, I could see the sparkle of humour, of gentle teasing. I'd never seen such a thing from Troy before. How could I resist going to the grocery store with him after that?

"Let's go!" I finally conceded.

"I needed a few more herbs for cooking," Troy mumbled while turning off the burner, as if he were suddenly growing shy again.

"No garlic!" Alexander relayed from the heavily shaded living room which had been dressed with black-out curtains to avoid letting even a drop of sunlight in at any time. While I thought that Alexander just may have been asleep at that hour, apparently he had overheard our plans—just like everyone could hear at least a little bit of everything at all times in that place—and had decided to allow himself a bit of a half-joke at Troy.

"Garlic is something I need," Troy half-yelled back, possibly not getting how serious Alexander was.

"He's allergic!" shouted Michael from the veranda, also having overhead us.

And, of course, also not wearing a shirt as he sat and read in the morning sun. I mean, why would he? Why would any of these damn guys ever possibly want to waltz around our shared living quarters anything but half-naked? That might allow me a moment to actually relax and think without having to stare at some ridiculously well-toned pecs and abs, and naturally that was just too much to ask.

"That's an understatement," added Kieran between bicep curls, also overhearing as apparently he'd been standing in the hallway just outside of the kitchen the entire time. "Alexander's garlic allergy, if you can even call it that, is about as severe as an allergy can get."

And of course, Kieran was also shirtless.

Goddamnit.

Closing my eyes and taking a deep breath, I summoned the strength to let go and ignore the stupidly tantalizing imagery all around me and just enjoy all the repartee. And it worked—I laughed a little out loud but much harder to myself at the boys' ridiculous banter.

As usual, I had to stop myself from laughing as hard as I wanted, but, also as usual I felt that to be the correct decision. I didn't want to encourage too much silliness. One of us had to be responsible.

It was, in many ways, all becoming too stressful moment to moment, but I loved the idea of getting out. I felt ecstatic as Troy and I left the flat, exhilarated enough to offer a chummy arm to him.

"What do you cook better than me?" he asked as we strolled down the boulevard towards the supermarket nearest our flat.

"What do you mean?" I asked. "I'm not cooking better than you. I'm not cooking *at all*. Well, maybe I've maybe cooked once, or twice."

"Yes, you are better and you know it," he continued. "I just enjoy the results too much to even remember to pay my compliments to chef Natasha."

As we walked further down the boulevard, towards the grocery market, it had become more crowded with Parisian locals and tourists. Troy quickly checked that his pointy fae ears were still tucked properly into his ball cap. As for me, I looked at Troy.

"You think your hearing is so much better than mine that you can just cover your ears?" I asked, almost without thinking much about it.

"Wouldn't you like to know?" Troy replied.

"You flatter yourself if you think I'm that curious." I barely had time to finish my rejoinder before he looked down, taking my cue that I'd annoyed him.

His pride was so easy for me to hurt. Even if I'd meant to do no harm, I still caused him some sort of agony, just as he and the others caused me.

We turned from the warm, summer weather and

delightful atmosphere of the street into the relatively sterile, air conditioned confines of the grocery store.

"All the signs are in French." I blushed, wide-eyed as we entered the cavernous, cheese and bread-smelling market building.

I mean, duh, but it was still my way of admitting that my French skills may not have been as fluent as my teammates'.

"You mean *Français*," corrected Troy with that same joking twinkle in his eye which I recognised from earlier that morning.

"Hmm, I never took you as the humorous type," I said with judgement, although trying not to sound too offensive. I would have liked to think I was just joshing him, as well, but apparently some of his usually endearing earnestness was rubbing off on me as well.

"You can learn a lot about someone just by observing their mannerisms." Troy's eyes still twinkled affectionately, even as he grew more serious.

It was an appropriate comment from him, too, as there was a lot I was noticing about Troy the fae that morning.

And for once between Troy and I, I didn't even have a response.

"Uh, so garlic?" I was almost tripping over my words. "And what other groceries do we need to stock up on?"

"*So cute.*"

I swear those were the words I heard Troy whisper, barely audibly, in response.

"Excuse me, Mr. Condescending, I was just asking about groceries, *s'il vous plait!*"

"Ah," Troy said grinning. "So you do know a touch of French after all!"

"*Français!*" I responded, walking away from Troy and towards what seemed like it may be the produce section.

Troy followed.

"You know I was just teasing you, right?"

"Ha, ha," I said sarcastically.

I was really feeling flustered by him again, as I was getting flustered by a lot of things at that time.

For the first time in a long time, I had half a mind to ring Emilio back in London, or wherever he was at that moment, to grill him about being paired with these infuriatingly sexy and just plain infuriating teammates.

Yet, I was taken with the atmosphere of the Parisian supermarket—the aromas of wines, cheeses, coffee, and olives, the unfamiliar yet charming packaging lining the shelves, the accordion music which I swear was playing over the PA speakers—that I dropped that urge from my mind and embraced the experience, grabbing an empty shopping carriage and pushing it down the nearest aisle as I let Troy catch up to me.

"Here, Natasha," Troy said, tossing a bag of rice into the cart I was pushing. "Just because you've never been to Paris before doesn't mean you should deprive yourself of the little joys in life."

Goddamn that sexy-ass, suddenly lighthearted fae, I nearly found myself grinning, and that was in spite of myself.

I had a job to do, for crying out loud! I was in Paris for the same reason Troy was there—and for the same reasons Alexander, Michael, and Kieran were, for that matter. We all had a job to do, and I couldn't let myself or any of my teammates get distracted.

Yet Troy kept showing off his apparently newly discovered sense of humour when "translating" the French signs around the supermarket.

I didn't really speak French, but I understood a few key words, and whenever he read one out loud, it made me laugh.

"Are you sure *danger* is the right word?"

"Oui oui," Troy responded with a grin like I'd never seen him sport previously. "*Dangereux*." The word sounded nearly the same in French as it did in English, and I didn't know what was so funny about it, but seeing it emblazoned on a shelf full of energy drinks made it difficult to fight a smirk on my face.

Especially when it was making Troy laugh so darn hard.

"Why would they call baked goods 'fat'?" he asked, while I nearly broke into a real laugh.

"*La matiere grasse*, Natasha!" Troy was just beaming pointing at a display of biscuit tins. "Butterfat."

I didn't know why it was funny, but boy was I laughing, out loud, louder and harder than I had probably ever laughed in a grocery store previously, and again it was despite my own conscious inhibitions.

I didn't know why I was letting myself get distracted by something so silly. I had probably let my guard down, but I fought the nagging feeling of that being unacceptable with the rationalisation that, as I had only fairly recently discovered that I was indeed an angel living on Earth, I was growing more used to living publicly and comfortably in the world with that knowledge.

The moment my laughter finally began to let up, and I felt the wide, giddy grin begin to relax and drop just a bit from my face. I looked away from Troy and tried to get myself together and focus on the task at hand.

At first, I had felt the usual relaxed sensation of having just laughed my damned arse off, a healthy feeling, but as my smile dropped even further I began to sense that something was off.

Quite off, indeed. As I began to feel hot, regardless of the air con blasting in the store, and tense again in a different way that was just, well, *off*. Like every one of my muscles was just starting to cramp up but stopped at the point of mild discomfort, I knew there was something wrong beyond just another poor night of sleep.

At that point, when it had first started, I was sure it was

some problem within myself—feverishness, an odd tenseness throughout my body, a general malaise that seemed to be sweeping me suddenly—yet as I turned my neck to look at Troy again, I found myself unable to move as quickly as usual, as if time were slowing as the air grew thicker with heat and the usually bright colours of the store grew brighter, with slight auras starting to rise and fall along evert surface.

When I finally locked eyes with Troy, I could see that sense of *off* was with him as well. There was a glazed, confused look to his eyes, and as we were sharing whatever oddness was starting I knew that there must have been forces afoot, the type of forces that we had both grown familiar with.

Indeed, a supernatural force was swamping my senses. It was like a tidal wave of energy, overflowing, covering, and permeating every single part of me. It hit me like a fucking truck.

I could hear the din of panic growing around me. I was not the only one who felt it, but the weird magic only started to grow stronger.

There was a rushing swirl of windy white noise, oscillating between deeper and higher registers so drastically that it made all of my nerves stand on end. The wavering between high and low had the quality of a panicked scream, and the terror it activated in me was appropriately primal.

And, despite the growing din of horrid, anxious static, the sounds of actual panicked screams had begun to cut through it all, with the high registered shrieks of horror and the stampeding of shoes across the supermarket floor telling the aural story that what was happening was real and it was happening to everybody in that store, at the very least.

My mind reeled in horror at what I could sense. It felt like something was ripping open a hole in the sky and a tidal wave of color was pouring out, bathing everything it touched in an unearthly glow.

Troy and I were the only ones left in the grocery store, at least that I could see, seemingly paralyzed as the glow evolved from a pale color to a deeper and darker red.

There were a few terrified voices still filtering in from somewhere—maybe still with us in the store, or maybe whatever was causing all of it was toying with our perception.

Whatever this energy was, it was taking on a demonic dimension.

2

LOST IN THE SUPERMARKET

Troy

I stepped protectively, although with some great effort as the air had become like molasses, in front of poor Natasha as the evil energy continued to flood through the grocery store. I could tell Natasha wanted to shiver, and honestly I did as well, as the aura the pouring over everything had was becoming a hellish crimson and the atmosphere was becoming frigid cold.

The floor started to vibrate and crack, as if the building foundation was breaking down.

Then, as the demonic power kept flooding through the area, stair-like cracks formed from the floor and ascended up to the sky. It started to become like a dream, or a movie, where I felt as though the feel of the ground beneath me was fading and I were simply floating, forced to passively view whichever images were before me.

From between those cracks, red lightning started to split the sky and rain poured down molten silver.

There were all seemingly mirages, though, as the apocalyptic visions kept shifting and morphing like a waking nightmare, much more vivid than any dream.

The demonic magic was fearsome and unfathomable.

My mind was overtaken with the occasional freezing cold which would grip the usually warm and pleasant place I came from, where I once lived long ago. There was no doubt that there were malevolent forces afoot, be they demonic or some other evil, playing with my own store of memories and likely Natasha's as well. Out of the growing swell of the buzzing, droning sound, I heard a deafening scream of monstrous proportions and the scene faded out and another faded in—almost as if the two visions were dissolving into each other—I saw a bright red dragon the size of the Arc de Triomphe swoop down from the sky and clamp its jaws around the Eiffel Tower.

That horrible series of sounds and images vanished as the reality of Natasha and I, subtly shivering in the cold in the empty Parisian grocery store flashed before me again.

The feeling of being near frozen yet near paralysed, the sad, empty spaces of the supermarket with the scent of mass panic still lingering—it all felt so real and was so real. Yet even realer was the sight of bright crimson then flooding every part of my field of sight and the sensation of being lifted then thrown hither and thither in a vast, empty realm with a formless red and orange glowing atmosphere.

Natasha and I did not land as much as found ourselves tumbling on a warm, dewy ground of dirt and unkempt grass. It took neither of us long to find ourselves upright in the midst of some meadow which, to me, was so strangely familiar that I almost let out a gasp.

What had begun as a routine trip to the grocer by our flat in Paris, had somehow led to Natasha and I taking a quite unplanned journey and ending up in a place I recognised but had never necessarily expected to ever see again.

The Kingdom of the Fae was an idyllic realm, widely

known—to those who knew of its existence at all—to be a place quite simply yet best described as being full of magic and wonder. At least, that's how I'd remembered it from eons ago—and until that moment I had assumed it was the same as when I'd last seen it.

As Natasha and I stood there then, as familiar as it was to me, it was also devoid of any life I could perceive. However, I recognised so clearly that we were not only within the kingdom itself, but I believed I had recognised the area in which we had found ourselves as well.

It was, or at least it had seemed, near to where the main palace was located, although the palace was not in sight of where we were standing—and wherever that was within the kingdom exactly, I could no longer recall.

It is an incredible phenomenon indeed, the way that memories of all sorts could come flooding back almost instantly with only the barest reminder of a time and place.

For me, it had been countless years, many human lifetimes since I had last seen the kingdom with my own eyes. Yet, before I could even consider what was currently afoot, the deepest recesses of my memory flung a vivid recollection of that palace into my consciousness:

The palace was made of black, veined marble, with a courtyard of similar marble paving around a stone fountain which, as far as I'd ever seen or known, provided a never ending flow of water. There were once bewitched lanterns that made the surrounding forest bright as day when the sun dipped below the horizon, but for whatever odd reason in my reminiscent vision, those lanterns looked long burnt out and badly decayed.

The sudden evocation of the palace in my mind's eye must have been influenced by the barren, desolate landscape which laid out before Natasha and I in that moment.

This was not the kingdom I remembered. Natasha was next to me, still shivering although whatever strange demon-created version of my kingdom of origin we were in was much warmer than that of the Parisian grocer from which we'd been transported. Instinctively, I grabbed and held the poor woman against me. I'd never felt Natasha that near to me before. Even in that horrible moment, it made me feel better.

"What is this place?" Natasha asked me, her voice quiet and concerned. "Where are we?"

"The Kingdom," I started. "It is, it was, in my mind's eye, an enchanting and idyllic place. There was, I mean, for long I'd thought if I'd ever see it again, it was supposed to be vibrant and brightly coloured flowers, and trees, and rabbits and deer prancing freely around in the fields. It was a whole world of nature, happy and free."

"It doesn't look like that anymore."

"No," I told her. That was quite obvious, but it was a moment in which it was understandable to not know just what in this world or any other to possibly say.

The Kingdom of the Fae was a place where such beings as fairies and pixies resided, as well as other peaceful creatures. The denizens of the kingdom, including those who made up my maternal lineage, were largely beings who did not die of disease or age in the same way as humans—thus my own memories being centuries old. My brain had held onto these memories for long enough that many of them lived in a blurry haze of idyllic nostalgia. However, all those eons of nostalgia would not be sufficient to provide the contrast between my personal image of the vibrant realm and the forsaken, desolate expanse spread before us in all directions.

Determined, in some sort of silent bond of shared competency and a stoic intelligence I believed Natasha and I both to share, we started along a dirt path through the fields of long withered grass, towards the visible turrets, over a hillside, of one of the myriad stone castles which overlooked all of this once beautiful land.

As we got closer to the castle, we saw that a large number of fairies were flying around it, laughing, floating, frolicking throughout the land and air. There was no relief on my part upon seeing this sight, though one would expect it. The gulf separating the somber scene we'd been walking and the joyful scene magically occurring defied belief because it was literally magical.

Surely enough, the vision of the joyous, playful creatures began flickering in and out, another demonic mind trick for sure. It was replaced by the continued reality of a barren wasteland, a kingdom empty of life, with the lively image even teasingly flickering in and out of view like a hologram atop the derelict castle.

As we lumbered forward, outwardly numb to the insanity we'd just witnessed, I could finally feel Natasha break our near-zombie-like spell of listlessness with the warm sensation of her eyes upon me. When I craned my neck to see Natasha's large, usually winsome eyes, then full of confusion and uncertainty, I realised that what I thought was stoicism on her past may have been the much more appropriate reaction of shock.

"This is…" Natasha began her question the moment we made eye contact, although she was not sure how to finish, I knew exactly what she was asking.

"This is where I came from, I'm still sure of it."

"But what was it like?"

Never had I dreamed about returning to the kingdom under the current circumstances, and especially not with Natasha. Yet, there was something inside of me that sensed that she could grasp my connection to that place more than anyone, and that she was also somehow grasping the pain which I may not have yet realised I was even feeling.

In that moment, as Natasha was looking up at me and not straight forward towards the castle, there was a sudden urge to take her hand, which I needed to nip in the bud. However,

I did take the opportunity to spell out some facts about the kingdom for her illumination and my own memory.

"All that time ago, this was a utopia…in some ways." What I intended was for a big, long, elaborate speech, conveying everything I could about the kingdom's past, about my past and what I knew, about what I thought was happening and what I knew for sure was happening, but the words only came to me in jagged fragments of thought. "Everyone was content. I saw no injustice or cruelty, and the forests were filled with all manner of magical beasts and plants."

I didn't even know how to continue. I felt like I'd just keep repeating the same sentiments, an innocent, almost childlike series of platitudes painting a fuzzy image of a home I then knew assuredly that I'd never see again.

I dared glance over at Natasha, just for the briefest of moments as not to forfeit caution to the dangers ahead.

Again, with a measured calm and only the hint of bemusement, Natasha nodded her head slightly. Whether I was projecting or not, there was a clear message to me in that nod.

There were more relevant things to explain.

Yet, as we heard the faint sounds of cloven hooves and claws begin to echo in the landscape, I still wasn't sure where to begin.

The place where Natasha and I had found ourselves thrown—from the inauspicious environment of a supermarket in France—was a far cry from the kingdom I remembered. It had been ravaged, surely, by the same demons or whichever that had brought us there.

There was a remnant of a dirt path which happened to be underneath our feet as we marched towards the large structure in the distance. While at first I had been certain that none other than demons themselves could have been responsible for the predicament my teammate and I found ourselves in, there was something strange about the way a series of dead leaves and fallen twigs were laying on the ground as we continued. The debris looked like it had been left there by natural forces, but there was something about the way it seemed almost consciously arranged, resembling some odd starlike symbol I felt I would have recognised if it had any significance.

As we passed the strangely-arranged pile of sticks and leaves, whatever odd, vague associations it made towards the back of my mind faded with merciful haste.

Our dazed walk of horror—in the possibly misguided guise of reconnaissance—continued in renewed yet even more absurd silence as the then much too familiar sound of demon hooves doing their ghastly work became more and more apparent.

While the monstrous legions were not immediately present in our sight, I felt my right hand—the very same hand with which I'd been tempted to tenderly take Natasha's own hand—was now clenching into a furious, tightly drawn fist of in bounds indignation as the demons' handiwork became sickeningly apparent.

Between us and the castle was a marketplace, or at least the site where a market once stood. I had not noticed until we were nearly stepping over the remains of it, much of it had been buried under the debris of shattered, scattered and burnt tree branches and all matter of other vegetation.

Walking, approaching the utterly decimated outdoor market, my stomach began to drop, firstly when I noticed the vestiges of lumber materials—the remnants of wooden kiosks—amongst the downed tree branches. However, what had made my hand just grip into itself furiously, and my jaw tender into a grinding furore was the sickening sight of blood, flesh, and nauseating gore.

It felt like less than an hour previous, I'd been stepping through the doors of a Parisian supermarket with my colleague and friend, Natasha, on a lovely summer morning.

In barely more than the blink of an eye the two of us were about to find a way to step around or over the remains of fairy folk, shop owners leading once peaceful lives, torn apart and left to rot like the debris surrounding them.

There was nothing that could prepare any creature in any realm to witness such a sight—except, of course, those creatures whose inner workings were wholly ensconced in pure darkness. The creatures whose nature was to dedicate their eternity of existence to the pain, destruction, and torment to any other beings capable of enduring their atrocities.

"You have not been good at all. You have not been good, and now you will feel the wrath of Hell!"

As the reedy voice suddenly growled from near directly overhead, I instinctively unclenched my fist just in time for Natasha to grasp tightly onto my hand.

That time, it was her idea, and she went through with it, not only clasping my hand with her own but gripping tightly and securely.

Smart move, Natasha, I thought to myself. *Now the beast knows we are united against him.*

It had seemed to make perfect sense at the time, you see.

As Natasha and I looked up at the floating, stinking, wisp of a creature above us, the demon hissed at us as nonsensically as he bellowed in guttural, rasping tongues of some sort before his words—quickly yet somehow with a painstaking slowness.

The winged thing was limbless and its entire body was a putrid shade of reddish brown, with jagged stumps for horns and a diffused orange aura that seemed to hang like an ineffable cloud of filth around it. Not wanting to waste the energy it would have taken to fight him at that point, I could tell by the looks of the thing that a touch of backbone would be enough to send him packing.

"Gone with you!" I commanded to the flying beast. Annoyingly, it continued to hover, fluttering overhead. I knew it had no answers, it had not a mind capable of such, and would only follow us and make trouble if we had attempted to ignore it.

"Go away, little angels," he crooked at us. I could feel Natasha bristle at his asinine, feathered attempt at sarcasm, her hand's grip loosening from mine.

"You know not what we are," I replied to the beast, speaking loudly to ensure it knew we would not fear a fight if it came to that.

"Angels. So proud and serious. We're just having fun up here. You angels always take everything so seriously." And with that, the thing flew off, back in the direction Natasha and I had been walking from.

Why he referred to me as an angel, I did not know, nor did I care whether he had mistaken me for such a creature or if he were simply playing some standard monstrous mind games.

However, I certainly appreciated the flying thing leaving us be. I may not have cared, but I didn't appreciate the way he seemed to mistake me for an angel, serious or not. I especially did not appreciate the way Natasha had seemed to slacken her grip on my hand each time he repeated the word until she'd let go entirely.

While it had somehow seemed like a safer and more efficient idea for us to stay hand in hand as we continued, I respected Natasha's wishes as a colleague and teammate and we seemed to reach a taciturn agreement to walk around the worst of the marketplace carnage, giving it a wide berth.

"Is it…him?" asked Natasha. She was not referring to the floating little gnat of a demon we'd dispensed with, or anything that was in our sight at the moment. In yet another moment of evidence that Director Hask had made the right decision in teaming us up together, I was able to intuitively grasp who and what Natasha was referring to with her cryptic query.

She was referring to the half-demon, Zavier, who we had battled only recently. In a previous mission, Zavier and his minions had insisted on making our lives a quite literal living hell with frequently disruptive demon battles, portals and transit between realms both planned and unplanned. Natasha was assuming, not unreasonably, that Zavier was behind this. "This all seems like his handiwork, but no, these are real demons," I told her. Zavier was half human, and likely still imprisoned the depths of the lower realm.

"No, I mean right there." Advancing through the lifeless landscape of my former kingdom, Natasha pointed towards the only other being currently in our line of sight, who I had not noticed previously.

It skulked, vaguely human-like, covered in some sort of garb of a nature obscured by the acrid air. From where I stood, I could only see a grey mask of a soulless, emotionless, face with two deep, dark chasms of black nothingness where eyes would be. Its appearance only became note ghastly and lifeless the closer it drew. It seemed to be walking in our direction without notice of us.

"No, that's also a demon, with no humanity I can discern. I'm not sure why you mistake it for Zavier, but perhaps I'm missing something."

Natasha's body inched subtly closer to mine as she tried to get a closer look at the ghoulish being. "I...I'm not sure what I was thinking."

Zavier was half human, and likely still exiled in the depths of the lower realm, humiliated by the defeat he had suffered at Natasha's own magnificent hand. We continued wandering slowly through the almost lifeless landscape of my former kingdom, but with the open, unobstructed path in front of us, we could not escape the sight of the demon, which was moving in some almost mindless, ambling way.

The thing had no humanity in it, a complete absence of any trace of a soul. It was a chilling effect that I could sense from where we stood no small distance away. Even that irritating flying thing had been full of life compared to the dead-eyed monstrosity glaring upon us then.

If I had ever seen a demon, the thing that was somehow accomplishing the task of sending a heftier chill up my spine than the other horrors, surmounting it was a demon indeed.

The demon saw us and stopped, spending an especial shiver up my spine to compete with all the gruesomeness I had just witnessed. I could feel its malevolence directed at me with focused precision. It was not Zavier, to me it was *clearly* not anything close to being human. Its eyes were emotionless, soulless; his face a stony mask. Grey skin and black veins covered the entirety of his face. His black nails were as sharp and long as swords.

"Go away, little angels," he said with a grisly voice, sounding so startlingly close in spite of its clear distance from us, repeating his demon comrade's words verbatim.

The continued talk of angels—especially in reference to both Natasha and myself—was mystifying and already growing quite irritating atop the unthinkable nighttime of an ordeal that seemed to just be getting underway.

It was a relief when the demon and its presence seemed to just evaporate into the horror-stenched atmosphere.

"Not Zavier," was Natasha's only comment, perhaps part of a slow realisation as she, like I, struggled to take so much in after being tossed into the Kingdom's realm like die from a Yahtzee cup.

We continued trudging through the near-lifeless world towards the castle, and it became clearer as we drew near that the building had no more nor fortifications nor even tenants thereof. It was indeed what we would have been considered a palace rather than a castle in the kingdom. It surely must have been one of the main palaces of the kingdom. My memory, even as old as my memories of the kingdom were by then, was starting to feel foggier than was standard for me as I could not discern if it was the main palace or just another one of the similar structures which I'd recalled.

Even in the kingdom's war torn state, the building itself was still monumental with a breathtaking regal feel to its architecture. It was something to behold, even as Natasha and I walked through the breached palace door .

Natasha and I began exploring the enormous old building with the same uneasy yet respectful quietude with which we'd walked there. It looked as elegant on the inside as it did on the outside. There was an awful sound traveling the brick walls of the palace. It was a groan of desperation, of starvation, pain and suffering. And as we silently walked the halls, clearing cobwebs from our path, the painful voice became a symphony of suffering, of the imprisoned, tortured and dying.

"What is that noise?" Natasha asked quietly although we were out in the open and likely not hidden from the dark forces who must have been nearby, if not in the palace itself.

"The prisoners and the tortured," I replied, feeling my right hand begin to clench back into a fist, along with my left hand that time as a crimson aura of anger flashed before my eyes.

"What manner of man are you?" I heard a voice from around the corner call out. *"A man of the light leads our rescue, yet you walk with him? You are a creature of darkness to do so!"*

"No! Please do not pass us, for we are blind and you are still gifted with sight! Please!"

The voices seemed to notice us, wherever there were coming from. They were spouting what sounded like jagged fragments of Old Testament verses mixed in with bits of half-crazed nonsense, albeit it was nonsense which may have made more sense to me when I still remembered much of the culture of the kingdom.

The trauma of the demonic ravaging of the fae kingdom ran deep.

"Who do you think you are?" a devilish voice, one that sounded very familiar, croaked near us, accompanied by a sudden, sulphurous stink.

It was that cryptic, soulless troll again, who Natasha had earlier mistaken for Zavier. Full demon for certain, although his look and manner were so familiar.

"How have you not been seized?" the demon demanded.

"Who are you?" Natasha asked, again demonstrating her fearlessness.

The brute did begin to resemble Zavier more closely as it deliberately stepped out of the shadows and closer to us. It was about the same size, at the very least.

"Who am I?" the thing mocked. "I am your leader and you will give me the respect that I am due!"

"You are no leader of mine, fiend." I took it upon myself to respond to that absurd demand.

The Zavier-looking demon's stink and snark seemed to shrink ever so slightly as it drew itself closer to us. Natasha had seemingly earned some small sliver of its respect.

"Call me...Kalgin."

After stating his name, the demon's intensity seemed to reduce even more, belying some amount of exhaustion.

"Kalgin?" I asked, not believing it was him there, a high ranking demon of inner hell, there in my former kingdom.

"Zavier's father?" Natasha asked, just as confused by the revelation as you were. "But Zavier was a demon, his name..."

"Was a fake one, yes," Kalgin told us. "I gave him that name to mock my own faults, my failings." There was no way on earth or in Kalgin's own kingdom of the lower realms that he was telling the truth with that oddly candid-sounding statement.

"What are you even talking about?" I demanded of the loathsome creature, sick of all it's word and head games.

Kalgin would have been among the last creatures in any world to make the truth less nebulous. His hellish mode, ongoing through eternity, would be to obfuscate, to confuse, and to put an end to any sort of lightness be it the light of truth or the light of life.

Kalgin began to grow before our eyes, shifting from his more humanoid form, either in his physicality or in another hallucinatory projection as part of some demonic mental warfare. With a slick, repulsive squishing sound, two horns pushed themselves through above his temples, growing rapidly and twisting themselves in chaotic swirls above his head. The black holes which made up Kalgin's eyes finally showed some presence of colour, but it was a muddy, brownish glow with an undercurrent of the white-hot flames of Hades.

I turned to look at Natasha just as the entire hallway, the entire place started to rattle and vibrate as if from an earthquake. Before I could see Natasha, before I could try to take in her expression to glean what she was thinking, we tumbled through a newly formed crack in the palace's outer wall.

At first, I thought we may have been sent through another portal, and worse, losing my teammate Natasha. Before I could even react I had already fallen several feet down into a slimy, muddy bog. By the continued echoes of demons scampering about and fairies and humans crying in pain in the distance, I could tell we hadn't been sent through another portal but were in the kingdom. I looked around in the darkness, frantically trying to find where Natasha had ended up.

"That was his father," I heard Natasha's voice murmur softly before I spotted her lying on the ground next to me.

It was if Natasha were trying to figure it out, or to

process another few bits of this ill-fitting puzzle from hell as it came together quickly and chaotically.

"Are you okay?" I asked her.

"I'm fine." Natasha demonstrated this by pushing herself up off the ground and helping to pull me up by my arms. I did my best to stand quickly as we needed to preserve our strength.

"What do we do now?" There was a genuine curiosity as to what Natasha's opinion was starting to burn at my mind with a surprising intensity. However, before she could even begin to answer, the sound of belligerent, hoofed footsteps quickly approaching from some nearby angle sent us both to run—near-simultaneously, as if we shared the same mind—and stealthily dive behind a row of overgrown bushes by the palace's outer wall.

We both ended up laying close to the ground, much in the same position as we were after tumbling from the inside corridor, as that is how we were least visible to whoever's unfriendly footsteps those were passing close by.

We stayed there, painfully still, until the group of clomping footfalls seemed to pass. And, perhaps to rest, we both seemed to have some silent agreement to lay still for just another moment.

"I never got to finish making breakfast." For whatever reason, that was the thought I'd felt important to share right then. I thought of the half-cooked fry up growing cold on the burner back in the flat in Paris. I even thought about how unlikely it was that any of the others had bothered to clean it up.

Natasha, surprisingly, chuckled in that moment.

"I'm sure our teammates just left it there."

We looked at each other, both still in the spots where we'd been momentarily hiding.

"I was just thinking that." The traces of a smile Natasha

had fell rapidly, and I knew it was time for us both to refocus.

"How will we get back there?"

"We'll find a way," she said, her voice suddenly growing much quieter. "But for now we need to get out of here." She gestured to the direction from which the footsteps came. I could hear them clearly again, and that time there was no doubt they were headed right to where we were.

Natasha leaned away from where I was laying, towards the edge of the bushes farthest from me. As she pushed herself up slightly by her left arm, it seemed clear to me that Natasha was trying to make a break for it—perhaps with the intention of running back across the open area from which we had come.

If that were indeed Natasha's plan, it was not a particularly bad one, despite the obvious risks. For one, there had seemed to be less demon activity in that area than there was around the other sides of the palace. Additionally, whatever portal it had been we had traveled through—whether it was a demon created portal or the less likely scenario of a magic circle portal created by fairies with dark intentions—it may have still been open somewhere around there, although neither of us had spotted any evidence of that after our arrival.

As the footfalls became closer, Natasha froze before moving any farther in that direction. She looked silently back at me, likely with some of those same considerations running through her mind and trying to confer with me of the best course of action.

While turning all of those facts around in my brain once more as quickly as I could, the decision was finally made for us by the sound of the hooved footsteps approaching from that very direction, sending Natasha and I to bolt the other way.

All I could think about was how we would likely be

spotted either way, and that bit of unpleasant logic inspired the perhaps less than logical move of leaping into one of the newly formed cracks in the palace's structure, climbing the rest of the way through the breach in the building's wall and finally jumping down into a corridor not far from where we had just seen Kalgin.

While I had been in front of Natasha, like any of my teammates I was aware she was more than capable of following me through that mild bit of acrobatics, and sure enough I heard her shoes gracefully hit the ground just behind me soon after I had landed.

While it was certainly no surprise to me that Natasha was able to follow me easily back into the palace, what I was less sure of was her opinion on the amount of intrusive I had taken leading us in there.

"Really?" Natasha whispered almost immediately, the harshness in that single word giving away that she was indeed less than pleased with that course of action. "Right into the demon's lair?"

A sigh escaped me then. Not because of Natasha's objections, which were not exactly unreasonable, but because of the conceit of the kingdom's former palace becoming, quite accurately, a *demon's lair*.

"You probably don't have to whisper," I responded, still using a bit of a whisper myself. "I'm sure he knows we're here regardless."

"Exactly!" chided Natasha as we began walking again, as we had been, down the empty corridor.

We had fled the demons outside the palace walls but had ended up inside those walls again, in a place that was likely no less dangerous, to say the least.

I thought of that half-cooked breakfast once again as Natasha and I began roaming the palace halls and the perfect idiomatic description of our situation became clear to me:

Out of the frying pan and into the fire.

3

FROM HELL TO ETERNITY

Zavier

*B*efore I had reached that insipid fairy kingdom, I had spent a year relegated to the deepest layer of the lower realm.

There, I had spent plenty of time in solitary agony, as that place was not meant for anything with human blood, and it served as a constant reminder that I was not a full demon by birth.

However, I would always be enough of a demon that a year meant the same thing to me that eternity meant, which was fuck all.

If the rest of my life was spent in the deepest pit of eternal damnation, I would consider myself to be lucky, given my lot of being cursed with sickening vestiges of humanity in my heart and soul. That was my mindset when I finally reached that fairy kingdom; I had nothing to lose. It was only when I arrived that I realised they were just short humanoids rather than the delicate winged creatures one normally sees in paintings and stories.

I found them disgusting.

They had the hearts and desires of the worst and most cloyingly saccharine of humanity, with unearned immortality and freedom from human suffering which could give the fairies even a modicum of character.

It was as if the entire fairy race had collectively committed the worst sin a creature could make; they chose to be boring. The rest of their nature was not worth mentioning, but suffice to say they were the lowest sort of prey.

Of course, I worked with the help of the competent demonic legions brought forth by my father, Kalgin. So refreshingly competent were they that I often felt myself to be like an idle prince of that revolting little kingdom, wandering the emptied halls of its former main palace.

What's more, Kalgin, who I had to thank for everything that was good and useful in my anecdotal makeup, had arranged for me to be freed from my boring and utterly useless time in the lowest levels of hell by allowing me to show my face again with the possibility of full demon status.

The opportunity was certainly alluring, but as part of the alleged ritual, my father had demanded the souls of every being—be that human or creature—he felt had wronged him. As one of the highest priests of the lower realms, my father would know what was required. But, like any worthwhile demons, his motivations were bound to be suspect.

Yet, whether working for my father's interests or my own, my days in that war-torn fairy realm were growing long and remarkably wearisome. My time roaming the former palace halls most evenings provided a pathetic excuse for the entertainment I should have been entitled to after a long day's work.

The fairy folk's architecture was bland and boring to look at, and even the cries of the tortured fairies and humans heard from many sections of the palace were bland and embarrassing for the insipid souls involved. Or maybe out was there annoying remnants of my humanity forcing me to feel that way.

That's what I would tell myself in my weaker moments when the pangs of guilt would hit me.

Still, the jobs had to be done, and all of those fairy souls and even sadder and weaker human souls were going straight to my father to fuel his own needs. I couldn't disappoint the old man now, not after he went through all the trouble of rescuing me from the damnation of eternal embarrassment.

Maybe that was another of the vestiges of human still within me, but that was a fate I had no taste for enduring.

I could still remember hearing his voice beaming in from some unknown direction and distance as I was in exile. It was not a voice I had expected to hear, but I would admit that in the moment it was a welcome vibe, and what it had offered was at the time beyond welcome to my ears.

Kalgin told me that he would rescue me from that fate, but only if I promised, naturally, to serve him as he demanded and fulfill the clear goals he would lay out. At the time I didn't dare hesitate. After all, he clearly knew what he was doing.

Good salesmanship was an asset in any realm.

"My soul for the pain! My soul to burn! Make the truth be known and my suffering to stop!"

There they were again, those asinine, nonsense pleas polluting a perfectly good empty palace.

"Shut up!" I wanted to shout to all of the tortured voices on one particularly grey and boring day in the palace. "Just accept your damnation and be done with it!"

Somehow, I didn't think that's what they wanted to hear, but they continued to wail all the same. Sissies.

Whilst I was spending yet another evening wandering, and yelling at the piteous mewling about the halls aimlessly, that the ground began to tremble. It started softly at first, barely noticeable.

And soon enough, it had passed. Immediately afterwards I'd stopped, out of sheer boredom and nothing else, to examine a tiny crack which had formed beneath my feet during the tremor. The crack itself was just that—a waste of time to even look at—but just before I moved on, I noticed something else on the ground: a thin wisp of ashen-blonde hair glinting in what little daylight there was. With some difficulty I retrieved the hair from the ground. It was so fine that I could barely get a grip on it. So fine that some would even call it 'Angel hair'.

She was there, I knew it immediately. And if she was there, then *they* were also there.

I crept through the halls as silently as I could, but the old wooden floors still creaked under my feet no matter how gently I stepped. Still, they didn't seem to have noticed me, engrossed in their own argument as they were.

I did my best to look disinterested and I was surprised when I turned the corner to spot them.

"Well, well, well." I smirked. "If it isn't fae boy and angel girl. Here to save the day, I take it? It's beyond saving."

"You," sputtered Troy the fae, with hilariously over-wrought anger. "I should've known it was you behind all this."

"It's his father," Natasha corrected him quietly.

"She's still the smart one, I see," I responded and laughed uproariously.

"Why are you doing this?" Natasha asked, finding her courage.

"Courageous, too, but maybe not quite as smart as I thought," I quipped. "To not only think that I'd tell you, but tell you the truth? Tsk tsk."

"You're making a mockery of everything!"

"I thought you guys would appreciate that," I responded.

"Why are you doing this?" Natasha repeated. "Whatever the congregation did to you, it doesn't justify this!"

"The congregation didn't do anything to me, sweetheart," I explained. "Humanity did. And I will never forgive the disgusting conceit of grace, favoured by humans and angels alike, for its hindrance of the rightful chaos of nature."

I was just making this shit up as I went along. Not bad, right?

"So, you kill, main, torture, destroy a world?" she responded. "You can't scare me with your grand speeches about chaos."

"It's not humanity in general I object to," I explained. "It's individual humans. Take you and your friends, for instance. As soon as the opportunity is right, you would feast upon human blood, if you could."

"That's not true!"

"None of you are even real humans. You're no more human than I. Yet you all insist on doing the humans' work of destroying nature, hindering its rightful path." There was no arguing with my contradictions or any of what I was spouting, and it was enough to start throwing them off from whatever tracks they may have been on.

"You're wrong! We want nothing more than to live normal lives!"

"A normal life is an illusion, manufactured by the congregation to keep you compliant sheep. However, if you insist..." With my angel girl before me at last, my purest and easiest route to full demon-hood, I stepped towards Natasha to make my claim.

"Not so fast!" With that obnoxious uttering from the fae-boy's mouth, Troy used seemingly every last gram of his pathetic strength and energy to block my path with an ugly-looking greyish-green forcefield.

Bad idea.

"How dare you stop me at the threshold of victory!" My

fury exploded, and with that my demon strength found a fresh source of sustenance.

I tore through the forcefield with ease and the only thing left hindering me was the renewed feelings of strength and determination coursing through me.

Apparently not even thinking correctly, angel-girl Natasha threw a fist in my direction. Not even a blast of angelic energy, if she could even summon such a thing, but her first. I clawed it out of my way—leaving just a mild bit of a wound which covered her forearm in crimson blood.

With an unsteady step forward around Natasha, I staked towards Troy to dispense with insufferable fae once and for all. He was already becoming badly drained as I could see him summing any shreds of magic he had in him to create another forcefield—and it wasn't even facing me!

"That's the wrong direction," I laughed before noticing it wasn't a forcefield at all, but some sort of portal to what looked like a crummy little flat from what I could see through the haze.

"Come on!" the fae boy shouted, leaping in as the portal began to close on its own.

"Is that the place the congregation provided for you? What a dump." I was having too much fun with the ridiculous display, regrettably not just grabbing the angel-girl as she stumbled around me, clutching her wound. "Mm, you sure, princess? I could still do some things to you that you might find objectionable… but in a good way."

Plus, I wanted to see if I was up to the challenge of talking her into staying. But, my attempt just led to a swift kick in my crotch from her boot before she leapt into the portal, the last of her making it in before it closed entirely.

4

FRAGMENTS OF A NIGHTMARE

Natasha

I tumbled to the hardwood floor of the Paris flat's main living area, straight back into the reality I knew best as if instead of being transported by some magical fairy circle portal, I was simply jumping from the bloody sofa.

I had long since abandoned the habit of falling on my bum in favor of a controlled slide, but I could've sworn that all these portals were getting harder to get through every time. My teammates were already gathering and turning their attention towards me.

"Are you okay?"

Speaking of bloody. "Yeah," I responded automatically, clutching my arm and already seeing a maroon pool of my own blood growing on the living room floor.

"Natasha, didn't you learn from last time?"

I had learned. It was why I was trying to keep the wound from bleeding out all over the place and looking like a butchered pig for my teammates to see. "It's nothing that a bandage won't fix."

I had to admit, I was a bit surprised when the rest of the team immediately gathered around me and started asking if I needed help. It was a rare show of concern. "Let me see," Alexander said with genuine worry in his voice.

"I'm fine," I responded curtly, my cheeks turning red.

"Let me see."

"It's just a scratch."

"You're bleeding," he responded, grabbing my hand away from the wound and looking at it.

Alexander's own existence had twice been saved by my own formidable healing powers, powers he'd seemed to have forgotten about. Yet, I could not find it within myself to be offended, as the concern he had in his heart may have very well been overriding some of the knowledge he had retained about me and our shared history in his head.

"It doesn't even need stitches," I responded angrily, snatching my hand away from him. "I'll bandage it myself."

"Natasha," Alexander said. "We can't just leave you alone. We're supposed to be a team."

Alexander stepped away for a moment, at first I thought from anger, but that notion was put to rest as he almost immediately began rifling through the linen closet for some short of sheet or blanket for me and my wound.

Michael, trying to hide the modicum of earnest concern in his eyes, tried to query us the best way he knew how. "So, Troy, you gonna tell us what the hell happened or did some unearthly cat get your tongue?"

It must have been a bewildering sight indeed to see that magical fairy portal forming in the midst of the flat before Troy and I had tumbled back in. As far as the rest of the team knew we'd just been out grocery shopping!

"Uh..." It was not common to hear Troy hesitate like that —the man did not typically speak until he was sure he had something to say—but he was probably a bit taken aback at his own ability to use his spritely powers to transport us from the fairy kingdom realm back to the team's flat in Paris.

I clutched my arm, trying not to dig into the wound Zavier had left as Michael tried in his way to lighten the mood. The wound felt warm and wet, but I didn't want to look at it. I just wanted to get the first aid kit and disinfect it and bandage it up before it started bleeding through the shirt.

"It looks pretty nasty there, Natasha, not exactly a scratch," Alexander said, pointing to my wound as he set the pile of sheets on the coffee table.

Kieran, gazing upon me as the rest were, wasn't the only one to remain silent thus far. While each of my teammate's belied some degree of concern in their face, Kieran seemed to be breathing noticeably heavier, his face growing flush with what I could only assume to be anger.

Kieran remained wordless as Troy continued to attempt explaining what we'd just been through. "You...uh, you might want to sit down for this. It's a little strange. Uh, we were in the store and then there was a portal in the produce section..."

"Portal in the produce section?" Michael asked, wearing an attempt at a mischievous grin on his trickster face which came across as of a pained simper.

"It was more of a hellish magic filling the supermarket," I breathed as Alexander wrapped my wound.

"I thought I'd heard screaming from somewhere nearby," Alexander commented. "It awoke me from my slumber."

Kieran, who seemed to be wearing a scowl on his face, still silently fuming, gave me a mild when I looked to him to confirm Alexander's observation. After all, he had the keenest hearing of all of us, and would likely have sensed such a commotion even from a few blocks away.

"Well, that clears everything right up," Michael quipped, causing me to shoot a dirty look in his direction. As I caught

Michael's eyes I noticed a degree of softness I hardly ever noticed there. Rather than trying to bury the situation in ironic attachment, he seemed, just maybe, to be more interested in cheering me the best way he knew how.

Alexander left my arm wrapped tightly in a queen-sized sheet printed with powder blue tulips. "That's curious," he observed, looking down at the sheet which had yet to be stained by more than a drop of two of blood.

"What is?" I asked Alexander, my eyes wide, trying not to laugh.

"I'm off to make some tea," was all he replied. I was still not sure about my angelic healing powers, or had forgotten, or was still ignorant of the scope of my capabilities.

At any rate, I decided not to question the wisdom behind his actions. Troy then tried to explain our mysterious, unplanned sojourn to the devastated Kingdom of the Fae and our run-ins with both Kalgin and Zavier.

"We were close to the produce," Troy began as I lifted myself up to the sofa, causing Alexander to stop dead in his tracks as he carried the fresh mug of tea back from the kitchenette. I was using my injured arm after all.

"We were just picking up ingredients, cooking supplies, having a bit of a laugh at all the French signs..." As Troy continued, I felt myself blush mildly at that detail.

"Well, it was chaos, out of nowhere, like a massive earthquake, horrid visions, then endless falling for Natasha and I until we ended up in my old home. The kingdom. Now war-torn, devastated."

Troy's voice started to break at the recent remembrance of the horrors we'd both been witness to, and my own eyes began to cloud with tears. I gently lifted my bandaged arm to place a hand on Troy's shoulder.

"Natasha!" Alexander cried as he saw me moving the arm. I smiled lightly at him and pulled the bandage off with a single tug, revealing that it had healed that point to a mere scratch, if that.

The others seemed amazed, but my attention was drawn to trying to finish the story as Troy could not go on.

"We've seen certain...things, I'm aware," I began. "But the way they'd left Troy's old kingdom, I never thought I'd see something like..." I almost found myself unable to continue. Seeing all that gore, the remains of the fairy folk scattered in front of the castle, I'd just felt numbness seeing it, but the awfulness was just starting to hit me.

"They?" Kieran snarled, speaking at last as his furor grew.

"Zavier," I answered softly, almost whispering.

"It was not just him." Troy had gotten it together, sitting upright as my hand slid off his back. "It was Kalgin."

"Real demons." Alexander's voice was booming, suddenly, as the realization hit him that our team had, for one reason or number, drawn the attention of demon legions which made Zavier's hobbled-together army look like a band of misfit amateurs.

"I remember seeing the symbols," Troy continued. "I didn't know who had left them, I thought they were certain fairies that worked for similar means as the demons." Troy went on to describe these markings he was referring to, which I was not sure I had noticed myself.

"It was an upside down pentagram," he said, raising his hand as if to draw it in the air. "But it had three points, not five. It was also red and black, with what I think was blood at the tip of each."

"Oh my god..." It was only then that I saw it. "But, some of them were..."

"Pentagrams," Troy continued. "Just straight demonic markings."

It was only in my mind's eye, in some memory of the worst of the horrors that seemed even more vivid than it was at the time. There were etchings of the tri-pointed star left on the ground, in the remains of the market stalls, and even carved into the palace walls. It was like some nightmare, fragments of it coming to me as if for the first time.

"Did…" I breathed softly, trying to think of the right way to even answer all the questions.

"I don't remember," answered Troy. "Or I'm not sure, but, it's clear to me now that it was the dark fairy symbol."

"Demons," Alexander repeated, standing up and raising his hands to the ceiling. "Don't let them deceive."

There was only one thing for this, I realised. "Emilio," I stated simply.

It would be necessary for us to inform him of everything regardless, but we all knew Director Emilio Hask would surely be able to provide some answers where our own knowledge and speculation had failed.

The flat's landline telephone sat next to the official 'business' laptop provided by the congregation on the coffee table near where we all happened to be gathered in the main living space.

Without another word, I switched the phone to speaker mode and dialled Emilio Hask. My teammates and I sat in silence as we listened to the phone ring. Emilio was currently in Rome, and while he was still very much working there, that knowledge added to the tense uncertainty that he would answer, a tension I could feel as soon as I heard the dial tone.

"What is it?" Emilio answered after two rings. "I'm on speaker, aren't I?"

"Yes, you are," I began immediately. "Do you have any idea what just happened to Troy and me?"

There was a long pause as we could barely hear Emilio take in a deep breath through the phone.

He was putting something together, and not surprisingly he was working with a breathtaking quickness.

"I heard about some strangeness in Paris on the news here," the Director stated, finally. "Just a minute." There was some shuffling as he presumably picked up another phone, followed shortly by a muffled yet audible voice in the background.

"Do you think, uh, it was a...attack?" the other voice asked.

What kind of attack? I wondered, as there seemed to be a rather crucial word we could not hear.

"I don't know. Um... I need you to look something up for me. In the records. The very old ones. back from... what's the date?"

"It was the twenty-first of December, year unclear," the other man said. "Why?"

The sound of Emilio furiously scribbling something down filled the phone speaker, and a small hitch in his breath told us all that he'd made a connection.

"Demons," he said.

"But, I was in the old kingdom," Troy began.

"Demons," Emilio interrupted, seeming to somehow know the story already, or at least the important bits.

"That's what they want with the human souls in Paris, and other points in Western Europe."

"We need to stop this," I uttered, my voice hoarse and raw as the snowballing of the day's event started to catch up with me..

"This could be the start of an invasion," Alexander surmised. While that much was obvious, Alexander stating it aloud put an emphasis on the dreadful urgency of the apparent, emergent events.

"That's not the worst part," Emilio answered dryly. "It wouldn't just be an invasion," he continued. "It would be... permanent. Unencumbered transit for the demonic hordes. They want to make all realms their own. They want to bring hell to Earth. It's an invasion, no doubt about that, but that word is nowhere near enough to describe what would be in store. What seems like... may already be in store.

"What do we do?" I asked as a tidal wave of nausea and acute physical panic rolled through me.

There was more pen scribbling through the phone line as Emilio was clearly on his way to trying to continue figuring this out.

"Stay one step ahead of them," is all he said.

"How?" To even my ears my voice was sounding desperately, almost mindlessly pleading, but self-consciousness was not exactly at the top of my list of concerns at that moment.

"I don't know. Maybe that won't be a problem."

"What do you mean?" Alexander was processing the news similarly, his voice snarling with uneasy wrath. "It sounds like pretty fucking big problem."

The disquiet of Alexander's guttural outburst hung in the still air of the flat as we heard Emilio sighed on the other end of the line.

"I'll need to get back to you on that one," Emilio said, at last. "Trust me, I won't take long."

My teammates and I looked at each other. We did indeed trust that it wouldn't take long, but it would still be one hell of a suspenseful wait before we knew what to do next. As if reading our minds, Emilio then added, "Start packing your bags, all of you," before hanging up on us.

We were all used to Emilio's cryptic messages by now, though this one was more cryptic than the rest.

"What do you think he meant by that?" I ask the rest of the group.

"Maybe he wants us to go on a trip," said Troy, half joking.

It had been a trip so far that day for sure.

Before any of my teammates could speculate or crack wise in their way, the congregation-owned laptop sitting next to the phone came out of sleep mode with a massage from Emilio. He was right, it did not take him long to start figuring it out. The message was an image, a map of Europe, and underneath was the text:

'Current Fairy Circle/Portal Locations'

"We need to ring him again," I heard myself saying, still trying to grasp some sense of logic or purpose from the entire mess. "That map is not enough to go off of, why did he bother? We need to know..."

"Hang on just a moment, Natasha," Troy interrupted, staring at the red dots on the map of Europe. The intensity of Troy's gaze at the image of the map was enough to interrupt my manic flow of thoughts.

"What is it, Troy?" I asked, slightly annoyed by his interruption for seemingly no purpose.

"We're not going anywhere just yet..."

Troy turned his attention from the laptop to us, and his stare intensified.

"We're staying here."

Clearly, I wasn't the only one of my teammates who took Troy's serious reaction to something he saw in the map to be, well, something serious. Alexander, Kieran, Michael, and I all slowly huddled around the map of Europe displayed on the laptop screen.

It was something the director must have managed to put together himself quickly from some connection he'd made himself. There were four red dots placed above reported portals in the continent, with a fifth yellow dot over Paris, representing the newest portal we'd traveled through in the grocery store.

"What does it mean?"

5

THESE ARE NOT RUINS

Natasha

"It means the end of days, that's what it means," Michael muttered in reply.

"No, it doesn't," I shot back with a frown.

There was something happening for sure, with Michael making what seemed to be a serious observation with no traces of his standard ironic defense mechanisms.

"Of course it does."

"Does someone want to explain what the hell is going on with this map, apart from the obvious?" I looked around at my teammates, growing impatient with how tight-lipped they were being despite the thoughts they all clearly had brewing.

"It's the end of the world," Michael continued.

Before I turned around to look at him, I knew I was wrong about Michael's sudden seriousness; I could hear the smirk in his voice already.

Indeed, by the time I had turned my head to suss just how sincere Michael was being, he had shifted his face into the form of American televangelist, Jim Bakker. "The end of days!" he shouted before laughing and instantly shifting back into his own form. "Just messing with you."

"You arsehole," I groaned, as Michael grinned with delight from getting me to swear.

"Yes, Natasha, I am," he agreed.

Rolling my eyes, I turned my attention back to the map, with the four red dots representing reported portals and the yellow dot representing the newest portal.

"The tri-pointed star," Troy stated softly, suddenly, referring to the symbol we both had oddly hazy memories of spotting in our recent sojourn to the fairy realm.

"But there are four of them," I blurted out, simultaneously with my realisation that Troy had discovered some sort of pattern, a constellation of sorts between the dots on the map of the continent.

"Five," Kieran corrected. We all turned slowly to look at him, all of us turning our heads at a measured, heavy pace, all of us moving with the kinetic slowness of a shared realisation.

"Four dots, and the newest at the grocery store." I began before Alexander had begun drawing on the laptop screen with a magic marker.

"You know you can do that with software, buddy," Michael started but stopped but when he and the rest of us spotted what Alexander had done. He'd drawn a pentagram between the dots on the map. "Oh fuck."

Finally, there were traces of real concern in Michael's voice.

"There's more," I continued, sensing it.

"My old kingdom we just visited," Troy interrupted me again, almost seeming in a trance. "The one through the nearby magic circle, there was a pentagram there as well. It was carved into the earth."

"Fuck," I grumbled, that evening's second atypical use of heavy profanity on my part causing the boys to all take notice and turn their attention towards me. "I saw it," I continued. "The pentagram in the fairy realm, and there was more than one."

"What was that about the end of days?" Alexander hissed at Michael. "Because this isn't a joke."

"It's not my fault!" Michael cracked back. "I didn't do this."

"Hey!" I interrupted, getting in between the pair of them. "We are all literally on the same team here, so everybody shush and let me think for a moment."

As my teammates did obey my wishes to shut their mouths for long enough for me to think, I did my best to start formulating some course of action.

I took a quick glance at the other points on the map outside of Paris. One location I recognised as being Madrid, and another as Rome. There was another dot over north-eastern Switzerland—likely Zurich—and the last dot was over some tiny speck of an island near France.

"We need to visit them all," I said.

"What?" both Michael and Alexander asked in unison.

"It's the only logical course of action," I continued. "And that's also what Emilio meant by going on a trip. I'm sure of it."

"Five of us," Kieran added. "And five fairy circles." He was already busy typing at the laptop, messaging Emilio. "Oh, and it seems that Director Hask agrees with Natasha. More details to come, he says, but he wants us to do recon on the supermarket sight ASAP. I guess together, or..."

"We're not splitting up," Alexander protested. It seemed as though the team were agreeing with my plan at least. "If we're going, then we're all going together."

Alexander had a point; though I didn't especially want to visit every location on the map alone, the team going together would pose its own set of risks.

I remembered the last time we were split up and I fell

under the spell of a siren in Sicily. While everything eventually turned out okay, I was still a bit hesitant to go through an adventure quite that intense again.

By the way the boys all turned to me right then, it seemed they'd all, consciously or not, made some tacit decision to let me decide.

I did not question why that was. With the urgency of the situation, I made the call I'd felt was best.

"Alexander's right," I said. "And we are going through this all together for logistics, for safety, and so we can all go back to that supermarket to see what's happening to the portal to the Kingdom of the Fae."

To my teammates' credit there was no more hesitation once I had stated my decision and what supported it. The boys all started to move towards the coatrack and the hall closet, gathering their things for our impending trip to the magic-ravaged grocery store.

It was some action to take, after all. The enormity of what hung in the balance, the souls who were already suffering, and biblical proportions of what was potentially afoot seemed to be filling the air of the flat with a shared solemnity and a sense of staggering purpose and responsibility.

"At least the first stop is an easy walk away," I commented. The central Parisian supermarket where Troy and I had fallen through the portal to the fae kingdom was the obvious first place to venture, and any doubt about such had been removed by the director's explicit instructions.

Fortunately, it was also getting dark enough that Alexander could travel with us safely. When the five of us finished silently descending the building's old, dark stairwell and emerged into the Parisian evening, the atmosphere was dark and quiet, with an unseasonable chill—and possibly news of the earlier chaos which had rocked the neighbourhood—keeping the usual crowds at bay.

The walk to the supermarket was tense and quiet. Going

by our past experience dealing with these same forces, I could not help but feel as though we were walking straight into some trap, even though we knew that Director Emilio Hask would not have even planted the seed of such a plan in our minds of he weren't positive that it was currently the best course of action.

"It's at the end of this street," I said, meaninglessly. After I let out that bit of anxious chatter as we strolled as casually as we could through the cool Paris evening air, I half expected Troy, who had just been there with me that day, to say something like 'I know'.

Instead, Troy lay a gentle hand on my shoulder, reassuring me. Instead of communicating *'I know'* he instead sent the much better message of *'I know, we are all nervous'.*

We quickened our pace to a march, finally reaching the supermarket's sliding doors. I expected them to be locked, but they give way with ease from nothing more than a simple push.

The supermarket was dark, and the only light I could make out was entering from the myriad of glass-paned doors, as well as the few neon signs advertising soft drinks that still managed to flicker through the darkness.

There was no lingering police activity or any sort of investigation of the phenomenon occurring. The supermarket was barely even shuttered off. It was as if the authorities were fearful of how to approach the situation. There were no proper lights on inside, and I was immediately struck with a sense of unease.

No, the supermarket was not particularly well-lit in its then closed and damaged state, but as my eyes slowly began to adjust to the darkness, I saw...nothing out of sorts, shockingly.

At least not at first. But as we wandered further into the darkened grocery store, it became increasingly apparent that things were still very far from normal.

The hellish essence that Troy and I had experienced earlier was still present, leaving a dim, auburn aura around many of the store's surfaces. The vaguely fiery glow became more apparent as my eyes adjusted to the dark.

But other than that, nothing looked out of place.

"It's a little creepy how quiet it is," Kieran commented, as earnest as ever.

"Yeah," I replied. "I don't see where the actual portal is yet. I do not love this."

"Of course you don't, you're much too angelic for this," Michael added with a little humour in his voice.

I shot him a glare. It was a heck of a time for him to be such a little shit, but he clearly felt as tense as any of us.

"I'm serious." Inadvertently I had lowered my voice almost to a whisper, an unwitting reaction to the ineffable oddness I could discern in the air. "There is something off, even more than when Troy and I were sucked into the bloody portal earlier."

"Well it is a market," he replied. "You never know when the store manager is going to jump out at you and tell you to get out, or as they say in French—"

"Michael," I cut him off. "I'm not in the mood. Hell, we have yet to even solidify a proper plan for..."

I was interrupted by an overwhelming sensation. My entire body quite suddenly began to feel that sense of...creeping otherness. It was as if every cell in my body was itching, or falling asleep, or on fire, or some horrid, conflicted combination of all of the above. The only thing that helped me stay at all focused and in some semblance of the present moment was the cold sensation of my fingers gripping reflexively into my palms as I felt a mood of balance and a distinct, deep drop.

And then, the drop ended and I was on solid ground again, dirt and grass.

Eyeing my surroundings, it took less than a second to

realise that I was standing in the middle of a clearing in a forest. It was dark out, the only light coming from the three-quarter moon in the sky above. I looked behind me to see that the rest of the team was with me. Alexander was rubbing his head in pain, while Michael was looking out into the forest with a look of awe on his face.

"Where are we?" he asked out loud, seemingly dazed for real.

"You know," I grumbled softly.

"We're back in the kingdom," Troy then answered, almost chanting it as the set of emotions that only this place could inspire within him washed over him as it had earlier.

"We cannot afford to stay still," Alexander started, looking up at the moon before turning his attention to me.

I nodded, not needing to be convinced of that. I looked out into the forest, taking a step forward.

"Let's go, then."

Troy grabbed my shoulder, looking at me.

"The state of this place must be as bad if not worse than what we have already witnessed. We cannot just wander. We need to think."

Troy looked over at Michael, his eyes betraying a searching uncertainty that was unusual for him.

Even Michael's usual trickster spirit seemed at a loss in that bewildering moment. Letting himself display an unusual degree of anxiety, he took a deep breath, turning his attention to the trees.

"We need to find the road, or something," he started, almost talking to himself. "If we can find the road, we can find our way back."

Just as he said that, there was a rustling in the bushes. The five of us grew immediately silent and still as we turned our attention to the sound and movement.

Out of nowhere, close to where we heard the rustling but seemingly out of thin air, a face appeared, followed by a small body. It was a girl, much younger than any of us or any creature I'd seen in the fae kingdom thus far. She had brown hair that hung over her eyes, which were a light blue. She was wearing a raggedy dress, and looked just as confused as we must have looked.

"Who are you?" I asked.

"I'm Amelia," she said, staring at each of us. "Who are you?"

"We're...we're friends."

She continued to look at us. I realised that she recognised us as creatures, foreign in one way or another from the ones she would know in the kingdom. However, I was growing impatient with this sudden, peculiar, slow-paced distraction.

"Where are you from?" I asked.

"I'm from the town over," she said, motioning her head to her left. "Why?"

"Are there any other creatures where you're from?"

"Creatures?" she asked. "You mean like animals?"

"Like us," said Kieran, finally speaking up. "Have you seen any of our kind?"

"You're not from here either, are you?"

The five of us looked at each other, and I looked back at her, waiting for an answer to my question.

"I saw a few people who were dressed really weirdly," she said. "They were walking around the town a few days ago. I think they were from some place called France, though."

"What did they look like?" asked Alexander.

"They had funny clothes," she answered. "They wore stripes, and the men wore beards... Wait a minute..."

She looked at each of us again.

"Are you from France?" she asked.

"We're from another world," I answered. "A world under attack by Kalgin."

"What's a 'Kalgin'?" she asked.

"It's...he's a demon," said Michael, stumbling over his

words. "But not an ordinary demon. He's...it's much, much worse."

"How do you kill it?" she asked.

"You don't," I said. "Or, rather, I don't know."

The five of us stood in silence for a moment. I could tell she knew that we were, mostly unlike any other creatures she had ever seen. Yet, she was not bothered by it in the least. A look of curiosity was written on her face, as she stared at each one of us, and her curiosity blossomed into awe when her eyes turned to Troy, who she must have recognised as a fae. Then, she smiled.

"How did you guys get here?"

My own eyes turned over towards Troy, as did Alexander's, Michael's, and Kieran's. Although he had not been a prince in that kingdom for eons, we had all seemed to deduce that he would best know how to address the girl, how to answer her questions.

"Well...it's a long story," answered Troy.

"We have time," said the girl. "We're not going to be let out for a while yet..."

Troy bit his lip, and then shrugged.

What did Amelia mean by that, I wondered?

We were back in the Kingdom of the Fae, for sure, having just fallen through the portal at the Parisian supermarket. Yet, we were in the middle of a forest clearing, at night, and this Amelia, wandering on her own, was talking of being trapped. Sensing that I, and the others, were bemused at best with this encounter, the former fae prince decided to do the talking.

"Amelia," Troy boomed, stepping into the clearing. "How have things been in the Kingdom of the Fae?"

"Not great," said Amelia. "There are demons everywhere."

"Well, we're going to change that!" Troy said, surprising me with both the boldness of that statement and a regal quality to his voice I had never heard from him previous. "We're here to help save you guys."

"Who's 'we'?" asked the girl.

Troy turned, introducing each member of the team, starting with Alexander, then moving onto Kieran, then Michael, and then finally me, Natasha. While I did feel myself blush when Troy said my name, the other team-mates and I just looked at each other, confused at the spectacle.

Like, were we supposed to bow or something?

"Where's Zavier?" asked Amelia.

"How do you know of Zavier?" Alexander asked, confused, as I believed that we all were by then.

"Things change," she said, quite cryptically, a bitter tone in her voice.

"Amelia!" A hoarse, guttural voice cried out from beyond the clearing. "You cannot possibly have reason for speaking with that ghastly prince."

From out of the bushes, a hunched figure loped into the moonlight. He was clad in rags and his skin a sickly grey. Behind him came more figures. Some looked close to collapse, others probably were. All of them were gaunt. The males were all shirtless, and the females wore dresses that were none too fresh.

The group of fairies were all disheveled and covered in grime that couldn't have come from anywhere but the most ravaged and war torn sections of the fae kingdom. Dark eyes stared out from an array of pale faces, staring at the team with a mixture of awe and terror. A few were brave enough to edge closer to get a better look at us.

"Who are you?" one of them asked.

"We're here to help," offered Kieran, as gently as he could.

"No you're not," brayed another, strangely aged-looking fairy, staring at us with baleful eyes. "You're with them." It was not clear who or what she meant by 'them'.

"We aren't with anyone," I replied, trying to be as nice as possible. "We're just trying to help."

"They destroyed our home," said another elder fairy. A somewhat more youthful fae, who to my eyes resembled an adult man, clutched their hand. It was not clear whether the gesture was out of affection or momentary fear.

"We're really sorry about that," I said. "We didn't know there were...people here."

"Please," he begged, his voice weathered and raspy. The sound made the skin on my arms prickle and crawl. "You're one of the good ones, yes? You're here to help?"

"We are," I said, attempting a smile of reassurance.

He did not look comforted. "We've heard that one before," he said. "They told us they only wanted to help too. And then they destroyed our forest."

"Who are you?" I asked.

"My name is Artois," he replied. His eyes darted nervously around the group, before he turned and started shouting in a different language. I didn't understand a word he said, but the others seemed to understand. They shuffled backwards nervously.

"What did you say?" I asked.

Artois's eyes met mine. "I told them to leave," he replied. "We don't need help from the likes of you."

Before I could query what exactly Artois meant by that, that jarring, discordant voice I'd heard a moment ago rang again from the back of the gathered crowd of fairies.

"Let the prince speak!" it bellowed. I had no choice then to look to my teammate and former prince of this kingdom, Troy.

Not all of the fairies seemed to recognise Troy, wearing only confusion on their faces as he solemnly stepped forward. It had been hundreds of years after all.

"You were a disgrace!" the voice shouted again. This time, the owner came into view. Wearing clothing made of animal hides and sporting a long, flowing white beard, he shuffled out with a wooden walking stick. He was one of the oldest fairies I had ever seen, which said something, and he stared Troy down with a look of fierce hatred.

"You were the shame of our kind," he continued.

It was Troy's place to defend himself, whatever his transgression was. Yet, as commanding as he had been just moments earlier, Troy just cast his eyes towards the broken branches and long-dead leaves beneath his boots in shame.

And he said nothing.

"Why have you returned?" the old fairy asked, his gaze still fixed on Troy. "Speak up!"

Still, there was silence. The other fairies seemed unsure of how to react. Some looked downright apoplectic, as if Troy had committed some grave crime just by returning. Many just looked afraid, not wanting to stir controversy.

I cleared my throat, trying to summon some semblance of a commanding presence. "Let him be," I implored them, surprised at how simultaneously tired and angry my voice sounded.

"Leave him alone. He's not worth it," one of the elder fairies commanded, building from my sentiment but gravely insulting poor Troy. Slowly, everyone seemed to relax, although the old fairy still glared at him.

"Bah! Foolish child," he growled, somewhat mystifyingly.

"Why are you gathered here?" Alexander queried the fairies as they let us pass. "Because, there are few places which are still safe from their shadows," one answered.

"They burned down our forests!" another cried.

Troy stood by, still under watch. The others seemed to wait for him to say something, though he himself looked uncertain now.

"They are bringing now the days of…"

"Our brethren are being slain by them as we stand idly here! We should…"

I could not make out all of their words, sadly, but it was apparent that they were at odds with each other. Their voices rose in anger, and I did not think that it would take much to have them turn on one another. I coughed loudly, trying to rise above their voices.

But my cough, and all of the long-suffering voices of the fairy folk were utterly drowned out by the monstrous bang which jarred the clearing and the entire section of forest around us.

"What in the world is going on out there?" a jarred, shrilly petrified fairy cried in response to the sound.

6

THE STENCH OF HELL

Natasha

"We've got to help." I started, racing forward towards the entrance of the clearing. But just as I reached them, one of the demons burst through the undergrowth.

It was an ugly, black beast which raced towards us with frightening speed. I only saw the whites of its eyes and the burning red of its nostrils as it snorted at us.

Its skin was coal-black but shone with a disquieting glimmer in the moonlight. It looked almost polished. Its arms—and it became clear as it drew closer there were more than two of those—were long and spindly, displaying an ungodly reach.

Everything about it made me think spider: The way it moved, the way it held its jaws forward like a pincer.

I was never a fan of spiders.

Before I could take in more details, the demon had leaped into the air, flying over our heads. I spun around, summoning the willpower to not let the beast's arachnid presence directly above my head distract me from summoning all the angelic firepower that I could without wasting more than a half-second's worth of concentration. I managed a small, pale white glob of effervescent power directed at the spider-demon's midsection. The fireball ended up grazing the bottom of one of its legs as it dove in for landing somewhere near us.

The fireball lit up the bramble around us, and I could see we were surrounded by a plethora of spider-demons. A weak fatigue bloomed within me from summoning the fireball, but it passed as I noticed that the demon who'd jumped was also quickly recovering from my attack, racing forward to grab me with its jaw. I had just enough time to secure the magic feather I had in my bag. I sidestepped its lunge, activating the feather into its sword form and sending a plume of flames into its rows of eyes before jabbing the sword up at the underside of its exoskeleton-plated head.

"Don't just stand there, Troy!" I cried, parrying a leaping demon who was lunging at him.

Troy managed to catch the hilt of my sword as I pulled it out of its body, spinning and slamming the flat of my blade into a trio of demons who brandished their own claws at me.

"Thanks!" It was surprisingly easy to fetch the handle of the sword as Troy relayed it back to me.

Troy leapt back into action, almost gliding into the acrid air with astonishing grace and speeding directly towards an oncoming battalion of arachnid demons.

With a proper weapon finally in hand, I flung my holy sword in a full circular motion just above my head to make work of several disgusting little monsters who thought it a good idea to fly, or rather, straight towards me using sickening little silky, slimy appendages to sail at my head. Before I laid them with a single swing of my sword, that was.

I used the flat of my blade to smack away several claw-laden limbs from my vision as I heard the panic of fairy-folk still nearby. With the wall of small demon monsters mostly cleared from my own line of sight, I could see that Michael had shifted into the shape of a giant fruit fly, which was enough to distract several of the dumber arachnoid demons to give Kieran time to pounce and tear their thorax-like midsections apart with wolf-like precision.

Stepping towards them, I dispatched what appear to be two of the last spider-demons, hovering nauseatingly in front of me, with two elegant swoops of my holy blade.

"Thanks, Natasha!" called out Kieran, ever the gentleman, leaping away from his newfound prey.

"No problem," I answered warmly, smiling at him.

Alexander managed to incapacitate the last group of the smaller-clawed demons in hand to hand combat without even needing to use his fangs, but as the forest clearing was finally cleared of the demon onslaught, it became clear that Troy took care of the lion's share of spider-monsters, tossing several of them to the ground from beneath each arm.

It also became clear that the fairy-folk had continued to watch, huddled together from a distance by the edge of the clearing. In the aftermath of the battle, there was a moment of silence as our eyes met.

"You've won this time," a familiar voice broke the silence. "But know that you are not welcome here, especially…him."

Well, this was just a pile of bullshit, I thought, and I had to let them know.

"This man, this fae," I shouted, pointing to Troy, just helped to save all of your lives. He put his own life at risk for all of you. Who gives a fig what happened however damned long ago?" I paused, staring at each of the little fae folk in turn. "If I were you, I'd be thanking him, not threatening us."

They stared back at me stonily, and after a long moment, their leader turned and they all shuffled back through the trees until they were out of sight.

"Well," Michael deadpanned, "that could have gone better."

"I know what needs to be done," said Troy, breaking his own silence at last.

"Oh, and what's that?" I asked him, my hands on my hips. "Maybe thank me for defending your honour continuously?"

"We need to rid the kingdom of monsters, now," he replied.

"You mean rid them of Zavier and Kalgin? Yeah, good luck with that," scoffed Michael.

"That is mad, you know that?" added Alexander.

"Zavier's gone," said Troy. "That's what the girl, Amelia, told us. I know the language here. It's the same but different."

"How can you possibly know what she meant?" I asked. "She spoke quickly and we didn't have time to discuss it.

"She said Zavier is gone. That is what I know."

"I don't trust Amelia," said Michael.

"I understand," said Troy. "But...she wasn't happy with the way things were run either. And she is wise. That's why they sent her to speak to us first."

"A *child*?" Kieran asked incredulously.

"That's right," Troy answered simply.

I looked at my teammates.

And she was there. Amelia. I almost jumped when she appeared. She was just there, by herself, looking at me. "Are you ready, Natasha?" she asked, her voice much kinder than before.

"Amelia!" I said, in a much less pleasant tone than hers.

"You won't need those," she said, gesturing to my teammates.

"But I do need them, sweetheart," I told her. I mean, awkward, they were right there.

"Very well," said Amelia. "They will never tell you, the elders, or anyone, but Zavier and his sire have left this realm. The others are too proud, or too dense, to ask for help. You can free us, tonight, from the shadows of the dark ones."

"Thanks for the tip. We'll do our best."

"Do your best to come to the palace tonight. They will be waiting for you." And she was gone. I turned to my teammates.

"Well," I noted. "That was weird."

"What was that all about?" asked Michael.

"I don't know, but we should go to the palace. That was just a warm-up, but the real battle's just ahead. I mean, I wasn't ready for it either, I still haven't eaten today."

"Don't change the subject," he said. I rolled my eyes and started walking into the wood and in the direction of the hills which I'd recognized from earlier that day.

It only took us a few minutes to make our way through the forest and to what remained of the kingdom's civilization. The streets were mostly empty yet full of disembodied demonic howling and braying, not to mention a sparse smattering of demons scuttling the darkness.

And I, frankly, was in no mood. "Stand back," I announced to my teammates, suddenly.

"We already heard your stomach growl," said Michael.

But, my teammates did as I told them, as usual, and stepped behind me to clear a wide berth. This time, it did not take much to gather a furious blast of angelic light and spew it forward into the demon-laden streets ahead of us. The shockwave travelled out in a semicircle pattern, obliterating the capabilities of remaining monsters before the heat and light ridded that realm of any remaining sight of them. I realized it was probably going to be the most powerful shot I could safely or reasonably manage that evening.

"There." I restarted my path through what remained. "That should do it."

"I'm gonna start calling you Ms. Tzar Bomba," joked Michael.

"Tzarina," I corrected. "And that was only a few demons. We should head inside the palace now."

Along with the brief wave of exhaustion which flowed

through me for a second or two after letting forth the blast of light, I could not help to feel a bolstering little glow of pride as I heard the footsteps of my teammates readily following my lead into this particular battle.

"Through the courtyard, you say?" asked Alexander.

"Yes," I said. "Straight through to the palace doors."

"And what then?"

"I don't know, rid the building of all those bastards and get home so I can finally flipping eat something?"

I led my team into the courtyard, which was still littered with statues from centuries of fae kingdom history, many of them defaced by the demon occupiers. In the centre of the courtyard was a large marble fountain, dry and cracked. In its moonlit surface I caught a glimpse of my own reflection. I looked pale and worn out, looking less than royal in my current state. This would have to change; we would take care of things and they could rebuild. Even if they continued to treat Troy unfairly, we needed him on our team anyway.

"Call out to them," I instructed Troy. "Let them know that we're here to help, that they can lower their guard."

"They'll find that pretty hard if the demons get to them," said Alexander.

"We can take care of them, too," I said. "Now call out."

Troy stepped forward and called out in a loud, clear voice.

"Hello! We are friends, newly arrived!"

We were greeted by the now-familiar chorus of the tormented, deep within the palace walls. There were some genuine-sounding cries of half-formed words, but it was becoming more obvious that many of the wails were ghostly creations of devilish powers, meant to perturb and disorient.

"Straight ahead," I said, my hunger and growing annoyance with the treatment Troy was receiving, motivating me to take control and get on with it already.

After passing through the broken palace entrance and

massive front hall, we walked into what appeared to be some combination of a throne room and a museum, a mix of gaudy furniture and priceless works of art, sculptures, and tapestries. And everywhere, there were paintings—Fae lords and ladies, famous warriors, ancient heroes from myths and legends. But the room was much too still, too quiet.

"Hello?" I called.

A scream came in response. Not the tortured scream of a demon, but the terrified scream of a human captive.

"Let's go," I said, drawing my sword.

We entered a long, dark hallway. In the low light, I saw a figure pacing in front of a cell. It was a demon, but much smaller than any we had fought before, its skin strangely pale and delicate-looking.

"Hello?" it said. "Are you more prisoners?"

Brandishing my magic feather once more, the demon guard hissed as the feather morphed into a sword with its usual volley of flame. Instead of fleeing, the dumb thing took a run straight for us, but I was just able to cobble the will for another small, white blast of angelic firepower aimed straight at its chest.

The guard went sailing into the cell wall with a quite final-sounding thud, conveniently unlatching and opening the cell door after smashing into it.

We looked into the cell. Inside, there were two figures, one huddled against another. As our eyes adjusted to the light, I saw a young woman with frazzled blond hair, matted like a nest of overgrown stress and suffering. Beside her was a similar-looking young man whose chestnut hair was sporting what must have been recently acquired streaks of grey running from his hairline all the way back across his scalp. The woman clung to him shivering as he stood upright, as still as a statue with glassy eyes staring forward at nothing.

"Who are you?" asked the man in a creaky, measured monotone.

"I'm Natasha," I said. "And I am here—we are here—to help."

"I'm Heather," said the woman. "He is..." her voice caught itself. Something about the story she was trying to tell, even as a mere introduction, was triggering some unspeakable horror in her voice and her eyes.

"He's my fiancé," Heather continued. "We were on holiday in Germany, hiking the Black Forest, then we were on our way to ski the Alps, just for a day. We'd been saving up. And William proposed." The young woman fought the best she could to keep her voice from breaking. "We were captured by the demons days ago. They've been... torturing us."

"We're here to free you," I said.

"Who's we?"

"My friends and I are dedicated to saving you," I said. "My name's Natasha," I repeated, hoping to create some connection of simple conversation to help the poor souls regain their grip on reality.

"We need to get out of here," bawled Heather, wild sobs rising in her throat.

"We must be quiet," I told her softly. "Demon guards may be nearby. Stand back."

I readied my sword and smashed the lock on another steel door adjacent to where the couple stood. The door creaked open, revealing a dark room. I crept inside, ready to fight. A dim light flickered on, revealing the ravaged bodies of men and women shackled to the wall, barely holding on to their wills or any semblance of energy to remain upright.

I brandished the sizable blade of my holy sword, demonstrating that my team and I were not only there to help but we meant business indeed. "Don't fret. We're going to take care of this."

"We need to get out of here," Heather restated from across

the doorway—much more quietly than the previous time, with an ineffably sad resignation.

"I'm William," Heather's fiancé stated, at last. I turned around to face him. "There are more captives in this dungeon. I saw them."

"How did you get here?" I asked.

"We were traveling from Stuttgart to Zermatt, by the Matterhorn. There was a train transfer, somewhere after the Swiss border. There was a delay..."

"Where? Which city?"

William went silent, a shell-shocked stare crossing his eyes as he sank to the ground and settled with worrying haste into a knee-hugging, almost foetal pose upon the ancient, gnarled stone floor.

"They have seen too much," asserted Troy, striding up behind me. "We can attend to them shortly, but we must unburden this place of these damned demons first."

With a quick nod, I followed Troy back out into the main palace corridors to join Alexander, Kieran, and Michael towards yet another battle with the monstrous pests still hanging about the kingdom.

"There are more held in the dungeons," I told my four teammates, stating the somewhat obvious while drawing their attention to the urgency of the captive situation. "Come on, we need to hurry so that we can get to them."

With that, I took off sprinting down the left corridor. Immediately, a trio of broad-shouldered, heavily muscled, bestial creatures came loping around the corner to meet us.

"Satyrs," snarled Alexander. "There really are only the dregs remaining."

"Satyrs," repeated Troy, readying himself to face the mangy beings as more of the loping, hairy, absolutely foul-smelling beasts converged upon the corridor. "They come to haunt ruins. These are not ruins, not by a long shot."

With that, the fight was on.

The satyrs gathered in the narrow corridor, and the moment the battle began in earnest it was clear they would for tough opponents. They were quick and rough, kicking, punching, biting, and stabbing the air with the sharpened antlers atop their skulls as they sped towards us. Summoning a slice of his dormant lycanthrope rage, Kieran growled and caught one by the throat, flinging him into the stone wall and falling flailing to the ground. The creature collapsed to the ground before Troy leapt upon him in a sprightly blur, ensuring the thing would be down for the count indeed.

Sensing the heat and putrid aroma of one of the satyrs attempting to sneak up behind me, I furnished my sword and, before the creature could ram me with his horned skull, I dove aside and swept his feet out from under him. With a cry he fell, and I immediately whacked it with the broad side of my blade to be sure he could no longer be a bother.

"These creatures...they're not very smart," grunted Alexander, hoisting the carcass of one over his shoulder and flinging him at another.

"I'd think twice before calling any creature 'not smart'," I reminded him, kicking out the knee of a beast and sending him sprawling to the floor, where Michael, having shifted into the form especially diminutive and unassuming, gleefully descended upon it to guarantee its incapacitation. "They're just following their nature."

"Nature can go fuck itself if you ask me," he grunted, slamming one of the satyrs into the ground with one hand and a second into the nearest wall with the other hand.

An eerie yet hauntingly wistful silence which soon followed, including the absence of the worst tormented voices which had peeled through the palace halls continuously until then. The departure of the awful din of sounds to the point where I could hear crickets chirping peacefully somewhere outside the palace walls, somehow sent a clear signal that the remains of the Kingdom of the Fae's demonic occupiers were, at last, defeated.

It was time to free all the captives we could, fairy and human alike.

"Looks like it's all over but the crying," Michael stated, agreeing with my unstated assumption as he looked around him.

"Anyone see any more of them? I'll check the cells," I said, turning to go down the narrow passage towards the dungeons.

"I'll come with you," Troy said, following me.

We searched each cell and room of the dungeon area, finding most of them empty, but others... others were definitely occupied. And we found one that still contained a fairy, even though it was empty of people save for one. In an iron cage was a badly burned fairy, lying on the floor with his knees pulled up to his chest and his face pressed between them as he rocked back and forth.

"Hello?" I called out softly, cautiously stepping towards the fairy.

As I stepped closer though, his head snapped up and he glared at me with a look that could kill.

"Get away from me, demon!" he hissed.

"I'm not a demon," I protested.

"Yes, you are! That disgrace to our former glory over there is proof enough, I can sense what he is, but the stench of hell still clings to you. I can smell it."

"I'll have you know I showered just, well...yesterday morning, at least."

I continued stepping towards the cage cautiously as the fairy glared at me.

"What happened here?" I asked softly, not wanting to upset him any further.

"Demons happened!" he spat. "One moment the palace was filled with music and laughter, the next it was filled with their vile demon cries as they began kidnapping my people to sacrifice to their infernal lord. I heard they also destroyed your palace, although you have already done so in many ways. Your kind are so weak to let such a thing happen." It was then I realized that the fairy captive was no longer addressing me, but was rather speaking directly to Troy, who responded by simply hanging his head slightly in what I could swear was a sort of shame.

"I am only here to help," he muttered. "I chose not any of this."

"How could you help by being the enemy? By existing as an affront to the kingdom?" Whatever in the world the fairy was talking about, Troy ignored it as he silently helped him stand upright, which the fairy did while still ranting. "There were some who have told me to forgive, to forget. I do not forget, they are forgotten." Now the fairy was speaking to himself, likely delirious for any number of good reasons, rather than Troy. Although it seemed he still expected a response. Ignoring his continued blather, I did my best to heal the fairy's burns with the threads of my angelic blanket as my team went to work freeing the other captives they could find.

"You're so young," he coughed, now speaking normally again. "But you carry an old soul. You have seen many things, unlike the rest of your kind."

Great, I'm being psychoanalyzed by a pixie, I thought.

"What's your name?"

"Natasha."

"A good name. A strong name. But it is not your real name, is it?"

I chose not to answer. It had become clear, if it were not already, that the fairy had no idea of what he was saying. "I was not always as you see me now. I... I used to be different. Just like you." He was beginning to cough, but he continued to speak regardless of his pain. "So much pain. So much chaos everywhere. The world... it's unravelling. It needs to be put out of its misery."

He groaned and breathed heavily. Even though he was physically weak and incapable of any malice I could not help but be on my guard.

"Oh? You think that do you?"

"Yes. I know what you're capable of. I've seen it before your kind came here."

"Care to explain?"

He simply smiled and closed his eyes, a bitter expression on his face as if the world itself disgusted him.

"I'm tired of running. Let them do what they're going to do."

My eyes narrowed and I felt a sudden burst of rage, one that even surprised myself. Yet, with an unsteady deep breath, I pushed down any brewing outbursts as the dungeon was quickly emptying of former prisoners.

Grinding my jaw a few times, I let what I thought was the last of my outrage dissipate as I followed my team up to the front hall of the palace where the freed fairy-folk and humans had gathered themselves.

"I'll need to wipe their memories," Alexander said of the humans who had gathered to one side of the hall. I recognized Heather and William, and other unmistakably human folks. Their exhausted, hollow eyes shone with gratitude as they regarded my teammates and me.

The fairies, however, were not so kind.

"Look what that bastard is doing now!" shouted a wizened voice from the crowd as Troy was summoning his might and fairy magic to create a portal back to Paris right outside the palace entrance.

Bastard, I thought, doing my best to keep my growing outrage to myself. *Really? What a name to call someone who just helped save all your arses.* As the other side of the portal came into view, it looked like the corridor outside of our flat, probably for safer passage of the freed humans.

"I have to wipe their memories now," said Alexander again, in an almost apologetic tone. "It is for the best. Ring Hask as soon as you get back to arrange for assets in Paris to help them immediately. How long will this portal stay open, Troy?"

Michael and Kieran had already made their way through, and Troy was just about to follow their lead. "A few minutes, the whole process takes quite a bit of concentration, and I won't be able to create a new portal until..."

"Just get these people back where they belong," I snarled, immediately ashamed of the way my anger was manifesting as the humans finally began to move towards the exit.

"I should have known," cried that wizened voice from the fairies, still watching the whole scene. Instead of defending himself, Troy just regarded his own people silently and sadly. "I told you how dangerous humans were! But no, you wouldn't listen to me!"

"Right. Well. At least we can live out the rest of our lives in peace," said another fairy. "Without a threat of human invasion for the first time in centuries."

Another voice exclaimed angrily: "Can you believe it? They're taking the humans!"

"Now, see here!" I began, stepping forward, feeling my cheeks flush with rage. "We're just taking the humans to the world they know. And if you think this was a human invasion..."

"Come on, Natasha," Troy interrupted, that oddly regal version of his voice slightly resurfacing—albeit with an overtone of downcast resignation that was subtle yet strangely heart-rending.

Especially in light of the cruelty his own people seemed determined to keep throwing his way.

"But..." I spun around to see Troy's hand outstretched

towards mine, the portal starting to shrink in size. As angry as I was, I would need to let it out some other way.

"Troy, please, just one moment."

"Natasha, it's done," he declared.

I could see the flicker of azure from his eyes, but could not discern much from the meagre few candles lighting the palace hall.

"It is of no consequence, my dear," he said with a sad smile as he looked down at me.

"But—" I started to say. He held up a finger to silence me. "Don't worry yourself with the past."

"Worry myself..." I started. None of this had to do with me, after all, and I found Troy's phrasing to frustrate me further until I realised he was speaking not to me but, really, to himself. As I took a step closer I could see the oceanic hue of Troy's eyes, subtly muted by that same sadness I had seen crossing his face several times that day.

After a brief pause, I turned back to the fairies and gave them a curt nod of my head. "Troy," I said under my breath. The denizens of the kingdom watched us, bemused. As we stepped through the shimmering portal, I tried to ignore the curious stares of the fae as we left their world behind.

I was the last to step back through to the narrow hallway just outside of the team's flat. By the time I caught the surreal sight of the crowd of freed humans starting to make their way to the stairwell, the portal Troy had created had already shut entirely.

Somewhere in the strange blink of a second between the fairy realm and the doorway to our flat in Paris, I had lost my grip on Troy's hand. However, I could tell that he was there, not far from me, because I could hear the sizzling of olive oil from the kitchen and I could smell the magnificent aromas of his cooking, sending my long-empty stomach into an intensely needy, greedy growl. And I knew that Kieran was there because he was already speaking with the director through the speaker phone.

"So these portals are just one-way?" I heard Kieran ask.

"Not necessarily," Emilio explained as Kieran scribbled notes down in an open composition book amongst the papers and printouts of the increasingly makeshift office.

"Did we do the right thing taking the humans back that way?"

"Yes," Emilio answered. "Because the fairy circle portals are volatile, depending greatly on the rituals involved with their creation and maintenance. But in your case we needed you all back in time to get some rest for tomorrow."

"What's tomorrow?" I asked, joining in on the phone conversation just as Troy walked in with my breakfast fry-up, for which I had been waiting all day.

"Tomorrow," Emilio began, taking his time to continue telling me as I heard papers shuffling on his end of the phone line. Alexander and Michael also chose that moment to enter the flat.

"The humans now remember nothing," Alexander said in a rare bit of breathlessness. "And we have handed them off to the crisis team."

"Good," responded Emilio through the phone's speaker. "Something told me we'd need those assets in Paris."

"But, what is happening tomorrow?" I asked immediately before stuffing a forkful of fried eggs and sausage into my mouth.

"Tomorrow," the director started again. "Tomorrow evening I've gotten you all train tickets from Gare de Lyon station to Zurich." While I was busy closing my eyes in ecstasy from the flavours of Troy's cooking, the word 'Zurich' had them opening wide again. That must have been that point on the map over Switzerland.

"Should I brush up on my Swiss German or Swiss French?" Michael asked, a bit too jokingly for the moment.

"Swiss German," grumbled an annoyed Kieran before Hask answered more appropriately.

"Neither. Apparently, this was the last train there all week due to some sort of police activity. We do not currently have anyone there to find out more, that'll be your job."

"So, no idea what's happening?" I asked, dabbing the corner of my mouth with the napkin Troy had provided me.

"Nothing even on the news yet," Hask sighed. "But I can tell you this much; Whatever it is, it will only get worse."

With that, Emilio hung up the phone.

7

THE NIGHT DEEPENS OVER FRANCE

Troy

𝒲hat if it had all gone differently?

Even after a hefty night and morning of sleep, the thought still had not faded.

As the baguettes had almost finished baking, as I sliced the bell peppers into julienne strips, the simple act of breakfast making seemed only to make my rumination stronger.

"You're awfully quiet," Natasha said, smelling of fresh lavender and bergamot as she stepped into the kitchen.

What if I had never been forced out of the kingdom?

"This is the first time we've seen each other all day," I answered with a light smile while pulling the bread from the oven.

Natasha had no direct response to that yet, and continued to watch as I opened the refrigerator.

I looked up from the fridge, where I had been pondering what kind of jelly to put on the breakfast toast: apricot, grape or blackcurrant. I knew now what I had to do, and for the first time in my life, I was actually excited about it.

"I really want bell peppers on my sandwich now."

Natasha frowned, a bit confused.

"I thought you liked just Irish butter on them?" she mused. As small a detail as it was, I was impressed that she had remembered.

Also impressive that she had picked up that I was making sandwiches for the team's train journey concurrently with my breakfast preparations.

"Yes, I do," I responded quickly.

"Then why the change in mind? Are you on a diet?" she asked.

"Nope, but I am getting old," I half-joked.

The truth was that I was getting old, even if aging did not happen in any traditional sense for me. We had both seen, just the previous evening, how certain lives could start to take their toll on even the fae kind. It had served as a reminder that holding onto youth in my mind, the spark of excitement and enjoyment of living, was key to holding onto the outward youth of my physical form.

"You've got your life ahead of you," Natasha replied sarcastically.

I had a feeling she was rolling her eyes at me as I started getting out the rest of the ingredients to make our sandwiches.

I think it was at this point that I started chuckling to myself.

"What's so funny?" she asked, annoyed.

"You," I responded. "Thought you were going to leave me to my thoughts for a bit longer?"

"You looked like you were deep in thought. I know how much you like to do that," she retorted.

I wasn't going to argue the point with her.

The sound of Alexander shuffling around in the living room, even with the blackout curtains blocking that space from natural light, served as a reminder that the day was already starting to wane and we would all be departing for

Switzerland, and whatever lay in wait for us there, before very long.

We had all gotten up at different times, but all of us in plenty of time in order to prepare for our journey, but it had been nearly an hour since we had printed the train tickets Hask had emailed us, and Alexander had barely made an appearance, little less said a word to any of us. This was very out of character for him and I wondered if this was some tell that he was especially apprehensive about what would be on the other end of the journey in Zurich.

It probably did not help that there was a sizable storm seemingly brewing outside.

Natasha continued to watch as I sliced the baguettes, uncrossing her arms and stepping her foot slightly into the kitchen.

"Something on your mind?" I asked her with just a flash of a polite smile before turning my eyes back to the knife and the bread.

"I was just noticing how foggy condensation has started to gather on the outside of the windows. The train doesn't leave for a bit, I believe; we could probably afford to leave a little early. Also, you know how Alexander prefers privacy when he wakes up. So if we moved now, we'd be able to find him his own seat on the train. It might also be more peaceful for us all, as well, have room to spread out a little more," she suggested.

"The platform will probably be packed like sardines just before we board. But we all have private sleeping compartments for the trip. We will all have privacy."

"Oh," I heard Natasha respond, and as I glanced out at her again I noticed her staring down at the linoleum flooring.

Was it not a good thing that we all had privacy? That is what I wanted to ask, but as I had no idea what Natasha could be thinking at that moment, I just kept talking to give a chance to reflect on whatever it was.

"But we will be arriving a couple hours or more before daybreak," I said. "We will have to go out and do our initial scouting of Zurich quickly." I kept talking, a bit more quietly, gesturing to Alexander in the other room. "Then, we may need to retreat to the congregation's accommodations until nightfall. I think I've heard the apartment there is larger and nicer. Then, once darkness falls we can go search out this place, and proceed whichever way we decide is best."

"Sounds like a solid plan," Natasha replied, before finally looking up and making eye contact. "But, if we need to operate in the dark, maybe we should avoid sleeping too much on the train. You know, sleep schedule and all that."

Immediately I felt myself raising a curious eyebrow at her. Natasha had been working with us and with Alexander for some time. This was nothing new and it was strange for her to bring up. Regardless, I did my best to keep a neutral face as she just shrugged as if to say 'just an idea'.

"If you want to play solitaire in your compartment all night, that's up to you." With a mild smirk I finished the first baguette and began making a breakfast plate for her. Natasha walked across the kitchen, seemingly impatient to get what I was preparing, and arrived at my side the moment I had finished filling the plate with stewed eggs, potatoes, and tomatoes.

"No cards for solitaire." With that strange comment Natasha grabbed the plate from the counter the split-second I could finish preparing it. "That's the problem."

I had no time to consider what in the devil Natasha was on about before a wide, radiant grin spread across her face. It must have been something about her angelic powers which sent a wave of unexpected warmth through me as my heart seemed to skip a beat, or two.

Maybe she realised she was not making sense so she used some sort of cherubic charm to distract me.

That must have been it. It had worked though, at least long enough for Michael to wander into the kitchen.

"Finally," he said, eyeing the breakfast plate I started making for him. "It may as well be brunch at this point. Or dinner."

"Saved by the bell," I said to Natasha a bit under my breath, and sure she would not understand the subtle joke.

Natasha's grin just widened even more, almost causing me to spill a spatula full of fried potatoes on the floor.

"Hey, eyes on the ball, chief," Michael laughed. Natasha giggled, seemingly at Michael's joke, but still watching me.

She must have been in a festive mood, I figured. Maybe as a way of dealing with all of the heaviness surrounding the previous evening and the upcoming mission to Zurich.

"You got it, boss," I said to him, rounding the bar with the plate.

Stepping a few paces across the well-worn kitchen floor, I handed him his breakfast. Michael's eyes remained focused on the plate. "Thanks, man," he said.

I eyed the meagre amount of food left in the pan—the food meant for me.

It was not as if I was very hungry anyway. Perhaps the nature of our mission was weighing on me, but all I could think about for a moment was my lack of certain memories of the kingdom, from my days as a prince.

There were things I felt as though I remembered vividly, but some other facets of my daily life there, like eating, what I consumed day to day, even the routine dining habits of the royalty there were things I could not conjure in my mind save for the vaguest ghosts of memories.

Spectres of memories so ethereal I could even be sure if they were real.

Chalking it all up to my mind's way of expressing my uncertainty and uneasiness regarding the massive nature of my team's mission, I forced myself to end that useless train of thought and walked into the living room.

Kieran was sitting in the old rocking chair in the corner, which I considered to be ornamental. However, he was actually rocking on the thing, a bit nervously as he looked through the printed rail passes.

"You're going to wear holes in those things if you keep obsessing over them," I said. "You must have every detail of those tickets committed to memory by now."

"It's an important mission," he said, shrugging his shoulders.

From where he sat, he could see through the tiny crack between the blackout curtain and the wall by the window. It was not enough to let sunlight in, but Kieran angled his head just right to catch a glimpse of the boulevard outside.

"It will get dark earlier tonight," he observed.

"With the clouds, it will be safe enough for me soon," Alexander said while rising from the sofa.

"The sooner we can depart, the better."

Kieran almost shot up from the rocking chair with a burst of anxious energy he had clearly been holding back.

When looked over at Natasha stepping in from the kitchen, she, amazingly, still looked happy and relaxed as she licked the last bits of egg and potato from her fork. "I'm ready," she announced with a smile.

Michael started shovelling his meal into his face faster. "Give me a minute, guys, sheesh."

I stood up. "No worries, Michael, I need at last two minutes to pack the sandwiches."

Natasha laughed again, and even that was enough for me to feel a little ripple of warmth and for my heart to not skip a beat but to seem to go faster for the briefest of moments.

While packing our baguettes for the train ride, I realised that Natasha must have been using her angelic charms to help lighten the mood of the team from its current anxious heaviness so we could head to Zurich confident and ready.

"Good use of your talents," I whispered to myself as I finished packing the food.

"What was that?" Michael's voice asked. I turned around to see the rest of the team all standing behind me, their bags, ready to depart.

"Nothing. I'll get my bag."

I walked back to my room and threw my bag over my shoulder.

"I would like to board early, before we have to deal with too many… passengers," I heard Kieran relay nervously as I walked back into the kitchen.

It was clear that he wanted to say 'humans', but as we were all ideally becoming comfortable in the world of humans as part of becoming more effective as a team, Kieran felt the need to stop himself from stating that outright.

"If we leave on foot now it should be no problem," Alexander responded as I arrived to face my waiting team-mates in the kitchen.

"Right then," I said with authority, growing weary of the team standing around and expressing their anxiety in all sorts of weird ways. "We have a train to catch."

Natasha, Alexander, Kieran, and Michael, who were all standing in sort of an inpatient queue waiting for me began to turn around and walk to the front door as I grabbed the bag with the sandwiches.

Outside, the Boulevard de la Bastille was quiet and uncrowded underneath the heavily overcast skies. It was ideal for us, but there was an eerie sense of electric dread in the atmosphere.

Arriving at the train station not five minutes later, it was clear that it was not only quiet, but unnaturally so. Instead of the standard echoing of rolling luggage and chatter of travellers one would expect at such a major transit hub, there was a vacuum of typical noise and energy I could almost feel in my bones. Along with the strange stillness of the surrounding blocks—including where our flat was located—I had to conclude that people were subconsciously staying away from train stations and airports, anticipating something bad happening there.

An announcement in French put a fine point on this, the voice coming through the PA system piercing the dead air of the station was a contrast that would startle anyone.

"*Embarquement anticipé pour le Paris-Zurich Express, qui relie Paris à Zurich. Tous à bord du Z-Express.*" The amplified voice was bored and monotone, as if the announcer had just awoken from a deep sleep.

"What track?" I whispered harshly to myself, ready to board the blasted train and settle in.

"Look," Natasha said. "There it is!" She seemed to notice the train for the first time.

The awaiting Z-Express stood at track *Huit*, a nondescript sign that bore its name on an otherwise blank red background. While I had expected some ultramodern train, maybe bearing some resemblance to a sleek bullet-type train one would see in Japan. However, the train that stood waiting for us was blocky, clunky, utilitarian at best.

It was maybe not as romantic as I had envisioned. As to why I had been envisioning anything romantic was anybody's guess.

"Express is a misnomer," complained Kieran as eyed the tickets. "It takes two hours longer than the midday train."

Kieran went wordless again as we boarded the sleeper car and he handed us each our passes like a teacher passing out a surprise quiz.

The inside was nicer than I'd expected, looking almost exactly like the fine first-class seats of an airplane. Soft, pleasant lighting and a gently curving wall led to a long hallway, probably where the beds were. Everything was quiet, and there was not another soul in sight.

"Put your bags over there," said Natasha, gesturing to a metal rack beside the doorway. "From what I have seen these sleeper compartments will be super small."

"Now what?" I asked, turning back to Natasha. Kieran, Michael, and Alexander had already started towards their compartments with their bags, having ignored Natasha's advice.

"Solitaire?" Natasha shrugged, smiling in a way that seemed mildly laboured but still with enough genuine warmth to be an oasis in the sea of unease our team had been swimming in for days.

I looked around the cabin, at the seats behind me, but nothing happened. Not another soul had boarded. It was quiet, save for the faint hissing of the release valves outside. The lights were dim and...

I do not know how long we waited. It wasn't long before the train slowly started to roll down the track, but it felt it.

"I wonder if there's an observation car." Natasha smiled a bit more genuinely before wandering off down the slim stretch of hallway by the sleeper compartments. I followed, glancing into the bedrooms as I passed.

I cast a cursory glance into each of the rooms as I passed, all of them empty save for the barest necessities. The beds were piled with softly humming devices that blinked and glowed with a comforting cool blue light.

It was cold in the hallway, and I could feel my pulse slow as my ears began to ring, and although I had grown used to it, for a moment I felt the discomfort of my pointy ears tucked into my cap. The lights flickered once, then twice, as we walked towards the end of the car.

There was a sliding door there, leading out onto a narrow walkway outside.

I opened the door and stepped out into the frigid air. The

wind whipped my face, and I could see Natasha smiling from ear to ear as she took in the cold. I glanced over the edge of the walkway and realised just how fast we were starting to travel as the train left Paris.

"Are we supposed to be out here?" I asked Natasha, feeling the traces of a smile on my face. She was having a ball.

"Probably not," she said. She put her hands up like she was going to do a handstand on the hand rail, but then she lost her balance and tottered dangerously close to the edge of the walkway.

"Careful," I said, bracing myself in the doorway to keep from falling over as the train rocked back and forth.

She giggled as she regained her footing.

"Come closer," she said, holding out her hand to me. I stepped back onto the walkway and took her hand. "Now slip your other arm around my waist."

Natasha turned her back to me and slowly backed into me. I wrapped both arms around her and held on as the train rocked from side to side.

At no point did I think to question what her plan was.

As far as I knew she could fly, and was deciding to share that with me.

Not even after she turned around to face me with a bright, mischievous grin.

"Now, we can walk safely," Natasha said with a wink.

It was not quite flying, but walking between cars in the manner that Natasha had instructed was a bit more exhilarating than I had anticipated.

"Whooo!" she shouted unexpectedly as we stumbled slowly, step by step, through the wind, and the track sped by just below our feet.

I could feel the vibration of Natasha's shrill, excited shout as I continued to hold her from behind in the manner she had told me to.

"Okay, you can let go," Natasha instructed me after we made it into the next car.

"Do I have to?" The words were, I believe, not audible to Natasha. Nor did I expect to say them out loud, and I was not quite sure why I did. If Natasha had heard me, she at least pretended not to as she looked up at the glass ceiling of the train car.

"Wow!" Her eyes widened at the sight. "I think we found it."

I looked up at the sky. The clouds had cleared, the moon was shining and I was glad that Natasha and I were here to see it. The moon was waxing, a bit over half full, casting a silver sheen across Natasha's profile as she continued to gaze out the window.

Her eyes darted toward me, and she smiled, but turned away as quickly as she did.

"One day," she said to herself, continuing to look out the window. "I'll be up there."

I laughed a bit, more charmed than amused. Yet, still confused. I did't understand where this was coming from. As far as I knew, we weren't friends. Not really.

"What's so funny?" she turned around to ask me, still smiling herself.

I shook my head, not really knowing how to respond to her. At least, not in the way she wanted me to. So, as was now natural to me, I ignored her and looked back out of the window.

As we rumbled along through the night, I felt Natasha shift in her seat to look at me.

"Why are you looking at me like that?" I asked. "We don't really know each other."

Her smile faltered, but only slightly. "Do you believe in fate?"

"No."

She turned away from me again, and I could tell our

conversation was over. I was glad. There were things I didn't feel like talking about. As I watched Natasha's reflection just below the semicircle of the moon as rural France continued to whizz by, I was okay with the quiet and our mutual comfort to be quiet together.

"Are you watching my reflection?" Natasha asked.

Alright, I was more than okay with talking as well.

"Maybe."

She laughed. "You were, weren't you?"

"Maybe."

She laughed again. "What's so interesting about my reflection? Don't I look normal?"

"No," I answered simply, unable to keep a smirk off my face. All I could hope is that she could not see…

"I'm watching your reflection, too."

Damn. Blast.

At least Natasha seemed to be enjoying it all, judging by her growing smile and the sparkle in her eyes.

"If only you could see what I could," she said, more to herself than to me. "Ah, well. Maybe one day."

I could only hope that one day wasn't today.

The moment Natasha turned around to face me, I could tell that hope was about to be dashed.

"Troy," she began, the smile falling from her face already. "Why did some of the fairies from your old kingdom seem so, well, old?"

It was not the question I feared she would ask, and I was barely able to suppress my natural sigh of relief.

"Well." I smiled warmly, calmly, politely, like a friend. "With some fairy-folk, how can I put this, the years alone do not age them, not in the same way as humans."

Even as confusion crossed Natasha's face, I kept the friendly, open expression held onto my own.

"What?"

"Hmm, I would say that while the folk there do not age

like humans exactly, something they have in common is what is in their heart, what they carry around with them can bring age to their face, to their eyes, to their voice."

"What they carry around with them? What does that mean?"

"They're not just fairy-folk who have aged, they are fairy-folk who have seen much sadness in their lives. Some of them choose to hold on to that sadness until they get used to it. They get so used to it that it becomes their lives, and they need it. And that is when the sadness takes its toll on the fae spirit, and the body, and the mind. It is unfortunate, yet not uncommon where I come from. There is an old saying about them and it is true: 'Even when a fairy laughs, somewhere a fairy cries.'"

"That sounds familiar."

"I am sure that it does," I replied.

"Why were they so ungrateful to you?"

Damn it.

"I can't say for certain, but I believe that it has something to do with their culture. I am not an expert on their culture, but I do know that fairy-folk have always been a proud bunch. Even when they are offered a helping hand, they turn it down, because they are too stubborn to admit their weaknesses."

"What are you talking about? Who was offered a helping hand?"

With a heavy sigh, it was time for me to tell the truth. But I could not, not yet. Without another word I walked alone back to the sleeper car, and into the empty sleeping compartment closest to the door.

With the train continuing to practically fly over the bumpy tracks, I laid staring at the ceiling, with nothing but the pale, blue glow of the sleeping compartments control panel lighting the whole room.

There was nothing for me to do that carried the least bit

of appeal when I considered it. I did not care to look out the window, and there was certainly no falling asleep.

With my head fixed down towards the carpet, I strode back into the cramped corridor, outside into the whipping wind between cars, and at last back to the observation car where Natasha was sitting still, staring through the window.

There wasn't anything to see out there but the blackness of the night and the occasional streak of lightning. It was just a source of some light, I suppose. But it wasn't enough to give a good look at her face. Even so, I knew what the expression she wore was going to be.

"What's up?" she asked at last, her voice flat and emotionless.

"Not much. Just bored."

She shrugged. "Me too. Actually, no, I'm not. The moon is getting dimmer, and I can't help thinking about my mother, about Gatriel. Am I even supposed to be here?"

My instinct was to respect Natasha rather than try to immediately comfort her. So I provided my real, honest thoughts. "I do not know," I said, and after Natasha turned around to look at me, I added, "But I don't know what this team would do without you."

Natasha just stared for a moment, no longer smiling as she had been earlier, and not exactly showing any clear emotions of any sort. Her eyes just softened very subtly before she asked the question I had been dreading.

"Why do they think you are a disgrace? Back in your old kingdom, the Kingdom of the Fae? What could you have possibly done, Troy?"

After taking a deep breath, I gave the briefest answer I could. "I was born half human. That was enough to do it."

Natasha stared with her sort of poker face for another long moment as the moon became brighter again through the train's observation car windows.

"That's not something you chose, though," Natasha began,

and I knew I would have to do her the courtesy of a longer explanation.

"Well, I guess not," I said. "I mean, it was just the luck of the draw. But I wasn't exactly treated fairly once my… hybrid status came to light."

Natasha kept looking at me with her serious face, so I decided to tell her everything. My entire story—from my earliest memories until this very moment on this speeding train—poured out.

"I was born into royalty, as you know," I started. "While the Kingdom of the Fae is largely an egalitarian society, the royalty is still considered important symbolically, and for morale overall. My father was not just a mere king; he was also the lord of all the land. All the forests and fields, rivers and oceans, animals and people that existed within his borders were under his domain. He ruled them all fairly and with wisdom.

"It was a good life," I continued. "I grew up with the best of everything. Food, drink, shelter, luxury. I had tutors to teach me reading and writing, mathematics, science and history, music, art, and a dozen other subjects. I had fine clothes—silk and velvet and pure gold lace—whatever I could want. The end."

"What did you want?" Natasha asked.

"What do you mean?" I asked back.

"I mean, I am sure you must have had some dream, some ambition, some desire. Did you want to be a doctor and help people? Did you want to play the lute, like in those fantasies of chivalry where the peasant boy becomes a bard and saunters into the royal palace?"

"I don't know," I admitted. "I've never thought about it."

"Everyone thinks about it," Natasha said, her green eyes looking deep into mine. "Even if they don't realise it. Otherwise, their lives are meaningless and wasted."

"Well then, I suppose I wanted to find the person I loved,

and spend the rest of my life with them."

"Did you find that person?"

"No," I admitted. "I found my friends, but not that one special person."

"Ideally, who would you want that to be?" she asked. "A blonde-haired princess?"

I laughed.

"One thing is for certain," I began, without even knowing what that 'one thing' was. Fortunately, I thought of it fast. "The royal life was never for me. That was decided for me, true, but it was never in the cards, whoever is shuffling that great, cosmic deck."

"Then?" Natasha prompted gently.

"Just someone who I could trust, someone I could love, and someone who loved me too. It's not much to ask for." I was hoping Natasha would get my subtle facetiousness.

"What are you on about now?" It seemed like she got it, or maybe not quite.

"The team! Look at us! We're all friends here, and we all care for one another!" My words were still a bit ironic, in some way, but it was clear I felt that way regardless.

"I'd rather not," she grimaced, her smile twisting into a frown.

"Rather not...what?" I asked, regretting whatever it was I was trying to say.

"Rather not look at us and see what we have. We just all spend too much time together not to have to form some sort of affection. But...that is all that there is really."

"That sounds horrible," I said, playing at being genuinely aghast. "Why would you not want to be friends with the people you work with?"

"I meant exactly what I said." I watched Natasha's expression to see how genuine she appeared to be. While she was stone faced for a second or two, she could not keep that up for long and a gentle smile, along with a few quiet yet sincere laughs, escaped her expression. I tried to hide my relief while laughing lightly myself.

There was tension for sure. But it was not between Natasha and I, and I would have liked to say it was not between anyone on our team, but rather from the relentless forces of darkness and chaos that seemed to have their sights trained on us at all times.

I could hardly blame Natasha for letting off a bit of steam.

There was a moment of silence as the train seemed to almost slow for a moment, in spite of the fact that we still seemed to be somewhere in the middle of Nowhere, France at an hour approaching what seemed to be the middle of the night. It was a moment positively loaded with questions Natasha and I both seemed to be keeping to ourselves. One question seemed to be how serious either of us were being. Another seemed to be what I was really trying to say, and what she was trying to say, and if they were the same things at all. As the train began to pick up speed again, and the blanket of stars bathing the eastern French countryside began to blur by through the observation car windows, I knew I could not let that especially pregnant silence last much longer.

"I do like everyone on the team just fine," I chuckled. "Just for the record." Natasha's reflection in the train car window, as clear as it had been the entire trip, showed a mild yet unmistakable hint of a smile crawling across her lips. "I guess I just think with the demons and everything else going on, it's probably best to keep work and personal life separate."

"But what if you're..." She seemed to stumble over her words for a moment. "What if you find someone...?"

"Then I'll deal with it," I said. "On an individual case-by-case basis." There was a brief pause, but then Natasha continued.

"You are aware that the demons can take many forms?" I didn't turn my head from the window, but instead gave a nod. "Good." Her tone seemed to grow more confident when she spoke again. "I'm glad you understand that. You seem like a nice guy, but one can never be too careful."

"So I've heard," I said, my gaze still fixated out the window, watching the dark countryside zip by in the distance.

It took another pregnant moment before we both, at once, began to laugh lightly, then more than a bit heartily at that slice of banter. It was the kind of repartee I do not believe Natasha and I had shared between just the two of us. It was, after all, the kind of blather the others on our team seem to be fond of more often.

After just a few all too brief seconds of laughter, Natasha turned around so I could see her face and not just her expression.

"It really isn't your fault, Troy. And it really isn't fair." Natasha's eyes caught mine as she tried her best to convey her sentiment. Yet, all I could do was look down at the faded pattern of the train's carpeting. There was not much for me to say, it had been so long since the banishment, and it was not something I felt it would do me any good to think about or consider more than I had ages ago. However, since I could not just let Natasha's kind attempt to heal some wound which I would just as soon forget existed, if it even existed, I needed to give her some response.

"I think it may be time for me to go get those sandwiches I packed."

"Yes, please, I'm starving." Natasha nodded with convincing sincerity.

"I'll be right back." I moved toward the door, but then turned to look at her one last time. After all, she had saved me and I could never quite get enough of her company.

"Hey, Natasha?"

"Yes?"

"I'm glad our team has an asset like you."

Her face widened into a smile. "Me too."

The train began to slow, and I headed off to get our food.

Walking back through the sleeper car, I saw mostly empty compartments at first, followed by two compartments with curtains drawn over the windows, likely occupied by two of our teammates as we seemed to be the only passengers on what must have ordinarily been a quite busy intercity route.

Finally, just before I reached the luggage rack where I had left the bag with our sandwiches, I spotted Alexander in his compartment.

His curtain was open, and he was sitting on the meagre chair provided to sleeper car passengers. He was facing the window, just staring. Alexander, like the rest of us, was processing everything in his own way, and I left him be. After grabbing the bag with the baguette sandwiches, I walked as quietly as I could back to Natasha in the observation car.

I handed her the bag, and we ate as we watched the countryside go by. I found it incredibly fascinating. Even through this route through the thick of the European continent, there was this atmosphere of stillness. There were no cars on any of the roads visible through the route, and there were very few lights on in any windows. It felt as though we were traveling through the eye of the storm.

Eventually, my curiosity got the better of me, and I began to ask questions. "Do you think Zavier found what happened to my old kingdom after he departed?"

"I don't know," she responded. "What do you think?"

"He will find out."

"Of course," Natasha nodded, confirming that I had not asked anything worthwhile, before taking a bite of her baguette.

Indeed, whatever I really wanted to ask or say to Natasha that was not it. And I did not even know what it was I wanted to say. So I watched the night become deeper over

France in silence for a while, while Natasha appeared happy to do the same. Eventually, I decided to try a new tactic, and began watching the trees and wildlife outside my window instead. It was dark enough now that I could see their silhouettes being cast against the darkness of the sky behind them.

Whatever any of it was, most of it was likely figments of a mind and an imagination that had been stretched beyond the limits of what it had been accustomed to over what had already been such a long, long lifetime. After closing my eyes for a long moment to try and reset my perception to something closer to reality, I noticed Natasha looking at me again, her eyes locked on mine as they had been when she tried reassuring me earlier.

"You are quiet tonight," she mentioned, her lips twitching upwards slightly as her eyes narrowed just the tiniest bit. "What have you been thinking about?"

"I was just looking at all the trees out there," I said. "And the animals. I could have sworn I saw a wolf prowling around out there just now." Her eyes moved past me for a moment, scanning out the window behind me and then back to my face.

"I know what it's like," Natasha said, scooting along the bench seating and ending up slightly closer to where I was. While I was not sure what she meant by that, I did not ask. And while I was not sure if she intended to then lay her head softly upon my shoulder and let her eyes close, I also decided not to bother her about it and let her drift off into slumber. I had had enough rest already. The gentle rhythmic motions of the train and the soft glow of the moonlight drifting down through the windows was more than enough to lull me into a deep sleep, my own head soon nestling itself against the side of Natasha's.

And as I fell asleep, I dreamed that night of happy times in my life. The times which I only seemed to remember in the haze of dreams.

8

LAST TRAIN TO ZURICH

Alexander

It had seemed like the train's journey from Paris to Zurich had barely begun when I had made a semi-conscious decision to sit and watch the scenery, just for a few brief minutes maybe, as a way to relax my mind and further tire my eyes for a few hours of sleep before we arrived.

However, those few minutes turned into much longer than that as I took in what appeared to be a peaceful yet bleak landscape, knowing not what lay ahead. It reminded me of my pre-vampire days in the English army when we headed to the continent for the Great War. It was a peculiar feeling then, and I sensed something akin to that for the first time in a century. As I witnessed the train crossing the Swiss border, I gave up on the idea of getting whatever few minutes of sleep would be possible before we got to Zurich. And after we sped through the city of Basel, I stood up at last to check on my teammates.

The two compartments next to mine, where I knew Kieran and Michael were sleeping, were both still closed with their curtains drawn. Taking a few steps farther down the corridor, I was alarmed to see the compartments next to those not only empty, but it looked as though they had not been used. The bed in one compartment looked as though it had been sat on, maybe, and the other compartment was completely untouched. Rationally or not, I was filled with apprehension for Natasha. While Troy also seemed to be missing from the sleeper car, I knew that Zavier still had an especial interest in Natasha.

Without considering how our entire mission may have been again thrown into chaos, I made my way through the door to the next car, which was slightly ajar. The next car over was made almost entirely of enormous glass windows, letting in the witching hour moonlight. At first, I saw nothing but two empty rows of benches facing the windows. Walking tentatively further into the car, I felt a reflexive sigh of relief as I spotted Natasha's blonde hair. I heard the wispy breaths of her sleeping, not quite snoring, and it was then that I saw her head was resting on Troy's shoulder.

Next to them was the insulated bag I recognized as the container Troy sometimes used to transport food for the team. Standing still for a second, I had to wonder how such a thing had happened. Perhaps they had both awakened, hungry, or Natasha did and asked Troy where the food was. And that somehow led to them sleeping next to each other. Somehow. Could not she find the sandwiches herself, I wondered. Yet there was no use in wondering, as we would soon be in Zurich with little time to spare. I decided to let Natasha get whatever sleep she could, and that meant not bothering Troy either as she was sleeping on him. For some reason.

I did let out another sigh as I watched them. It was not a sigh of relief. In fact, I was not sure what caused it, but I tried not to sigh too loudly as not to wake them up. Sighing loudly was not my style anyway.

I decided to stop concerning myself with it and headed

for the exit of the car. Maybe some fresh air would wake me up, despite having not slept. Sleeping could happen in the congregation flat in Zurich, I figured.

I almost instantly regretted opening the door as the cold air hit me. Also, and I was not sure why, but there was something unpleasant in the air. It seemed like all the tension and darkness that had built up inside the train was now outside it.

As I looked out into the night, I saw a horde of creatures running about on the other side of the tracks. They were far away, but I could see them very clearly. They resembled the demons I had seen the day before, but these seemed to have more of an animalistic quality to them.

"Holy shit," I heard Michael say from behind me, and I turned around to see that everyone except for Natasha had joined me in the doorway.

"How could something like this happen? Who is driving the train still?" asked Kieran, hovering just behind Michael.

"What's going on out there?" asked Natasha, still sitting in the other car as Troy stared out at the ghastly scene.

"Can't you see?" Troy yelled back to her, seemingly frozen in place.

"No, I can't see anything except for yours and Alexander's back. The windows have all fogged up all of a sudden. Like, really quickly."

"Well just come out here and see for yourself," he replied, exasperated.

Sensing something was wrong, Natasha got up and made her way over to us. As she did so, the train started slowing down as we entered a tunnel. The lights in the tunnel flickered on and off making it hard to see the other side clearly.

"What's happening?" asked Natasha, looking through the windows, wiping off the condensation with her sleeve.

Suddenly the train came to a complete stop and what we saw was nothing short of nightmarish. From every direction, people—and I mean people, not creatures—were running toward the train tracks as fast as they could. Most of them were falling and getting crushed by the people behind them. Noises of shock and terror erupted from hidden speakers in the tunnel. What we were seeing could not be real.

"This is a nightmare, right? Tell me this is a nightmare," whispered Natasha.

"I wish it was," replied Troy.

The people were all screaming at the tops of their lungs, begging and pleading for their lives in several different languages, but I could understand every word. A lot of the time the screams would be cut short as the people were either trampled or shredded to pieces by something we could not yet see.

It did not seem real, but at the same time it was all too real.

It indeed reminded me of my last few days of humanity, in the thick of wartime. Some of my worst days, indeed.

We stepped back from the windows as we heard something scratching on the outside of the train. It sounded as if whatever it was it had claws like fucking razors and a distinct lack of patience.

"What's that?!" exclaimed Natasha.

"That," replied Michael, "would be our welcoming party."

The noise of the scratching continued as the sound of heavy panting came through the speakers. The noise was so loud it was like someone was standing right next to us, aboard the train. I had never heard anything quite like it before and I had heard some pretty weird shit in my time.

"What the bloody hell is that?!" exclaimed Natasha once more.

"The sound of why nobody else was on the train to Zurich," I replied. Of course, the level of chaos around us must have been brand new or we would never have even reached the outskirts of the city.

In an instant, the scratching had stopped, all of the noise had stopped. What followed was yelling. Not terrified screaming like we had heard for a solid half-minute, but just loud and half-interested yelling in German. The lights in the tunnel flickered on again, and what appeared to be an engineer in a reflective orange vest strolled up casually, and stopped when he spotted us.

"Are you Americans?" he shouted in a heavy Swiss accent.

"English!" Natasha yelled back. "What the hell just happened?" she asked.

"We are not sure yet," the engineer yelled back. "There seemed to be a transformer explosion, but we got the power back."

"Did you not see all the people panicking, running in the tunnel?" Kieran demanded, his bemusement far overriding his usual shyness.

The engineer just looked confused.

"In this tunnel? Nein. Now, back inside the train, ja?" Incredibly, the train started rolling again. "Oh, and for your safety, the doors will now be locked until the train reaches your destination." He flashed a quick smile, turned around, and went back to whatever it was he was doing.

"They really don't know a thing," I said.

"Yeah, I guessed as much," Natasha replied, clearly thinking. "Does this mean everyone in the train is a…"

"That man was no creature of any kind," I stated confidently as the train picked up speed on the last stretch of track to Zurich HB Station. "He was human," I assured Natasha, as reassuring as that statement could have been in that moment, at any rate.

"He was human," agreed Troy, a bit surprisingly. "There is another circle of dark magic somewhere close to here." Troy had a proverbial thousand yard stare into the distance as the train slowed down on its approach to the station.

"Thanks, captain obvious," Michael remarked as we

pulled into the relative peace and quiet of Zurich's largest train station.

"This is where one of the portals is located," I reminded Troy. "Somewhere in this city."

"The visions, I mean." Troy still seemed to be focused on some unknown point in the distance as the five of us remained huddled in a circle between train cars. "The closer we get, the harder it is to tell what is real."

The train came to a stop. The surrounding transit hub was empty, as far as I could tell.

"This is our stop," said Natasha. "Let's go."

We exited the train and walked out of the station.

"Stay focused," I reminded Troy as we set foot on Zurich's streets, still quiet in the predawn hours.

"I'm trying, alright?" he snapped back.

The three of us stopped in the shadow of a towering glass box of an office building as Kieran fumbled with his phone. "Should we try to find the flat, or?"

None of us seemed to know how to answer that question.

"Ideally before it gets bright," I responded for my own sake.

"This map is not loading," Kieran complained, an uncharacteristic hint of frustration in his voice.

I had frustrations of my own to contend with as I spotted a haze of orange starting to form along the darkness of the eastern horizon.

"The sun will be coming out to play soon enough," I announced, trying to add a hint of wit to my continued reminders to the others of my need for self-preservation.

Two humans, locals by the looks of their business attire and put-upon expressions, passed us a little too closely for my liking. There was one man and one woman, on the younger side, maybe married and commuting together. They both gave me a flash of a puzzled glance as I stared at the horizon. However, they seemed to be caught up in their own little world, perhaps in the events taking over their city. Their expressions were those of worry, but not of dread. They knew something was wrong, but they likely had not been affected yet, not directly. I thought about what that engineer said, about the 'transformer explosion'. There was a way that humans had of explaining things in a fashion they could understand. How everything was a transformer explosion, or a power outage, or just somebody's delusions or some form of mass hysteria that was making people see and hear things they should not be seeing or hearing. But when these incidents begin to build and build, even the most skeptical of humans start to wonder. I wondered if these two were the types to immediately rush for their cell phones as soon as things started to happen.

"We are usually more professional than this," I heard Kieran sneer, the stress palpable in his voice as he struggled with the map on his phone.

The Swiss couple had started to walk faster, I noted, before turning back to my team.

"Are you sure about that?" Michael asked of Kieran's observation.

There was no chance for any of us to respond or even consider that because the still city air was pierced by a discordant symphony of brakes squealing, metal smashing and crumpling, and glass shattering and crashing to the ground. As we all spun in the direction of the noise we caught sight of a huge, white Mercedes cargo van in the midst of crashing into a row of parked Smart cars. There was hardly time to take all of that in before there was another loud series of crashes and bangs, coming from the opposite direction this time.

We turned to see a black van weaving and speeding down the one-way street the wrong way. It was impossible to know exactly what was about to happen next but the sound of screeching tires was enough to draw our eyes back just in time to see the white cargo van smashing into the black van.

The noise was awful, but we kept watching out of horrific fascination as the scene unfolded.

The alternating tones of Swiss emergency vehicle sirens soon followed, wailing up and down almost in an iambic pentameter of urgent sound drawing closer and closer. The police cars pulled up on the sides of the conflict, lights flashing, but nobody got out. We could not tell what was happening with the two vehicles just yet, but it looked like they were still moving.

I stood there for a moment more, unsure of who to help first.

"Let's go, before they start to question us," Michael suggested, perhaps wisely.

"*Es fährt niemand!*" I heard one of the officers exclaim.

"*Wie ist das möglich?*" another replied in apparent disbelief.

"There was nobody driving," grumbled Troy, under his breath. The officers were starting to visually scan the area.

Kieran seemed to be on top of the slight movements of the officers, of all the humans in the vicinity, as much as any of us. His eyes, and subtle direction of his nose, darted to the officers then in the other direction, presumably to where we were headed.

"Let's go, the flat is just blocks away," Kieran whispered, and we followed as stealthily as we were capable of as a team, walking away from the site of the accident. After a short walk, we reached the large apartment building that served as our temporary hideout in Zurich. No sooner had we ascended the stairs to the front door when a voice called to us from the shadows of the stairwell.

"You are very early," it said. We all recoiled at the sudden appearance of a dishevelled man with a thick beard and frazzled hair. He looked like he had not bathed in weeks. "I didn't even hear you come in!" he continued. The way he was peering at us made me feel like he could see right through me.

"Who are you?" I asked. "How did you know we were coming?"

"I am Henry," the man said, ignoring my questions.

"Your name is Henry?" Troy asked in a way that I believe startled all of us. "Really?"

"I know who *you* are," he hissed to Troy mysteriously. "I know of the threat you represented. That you will always represent."

"What?" I asked, having no clue what this man was talking about.

Glaring, I took in his appearance: long, unkempt black hair and a beard of the same colour with hints of grey. Also, disheveled and filthy clothing that was probably white at one time. Upon further inspection, his garb did not appear to be modern in any way I could discern, nor did it seem to be from any earthly past era.

"Don't play dumb with me, Alexander," he went on interrupted. It was a vanishingly rare moment in which I needed to conceal a bolt of alarm I felt.

"How do you know who I am?"

"He does not," Troy interrupted.

"The enemy of my enemy is my friend," Henry said simply. Just infuriatingly fucking simply and meaninglessly.

"Who are you?" I asked again.

"I told you," he said shortly. "I am Henry."

"No!" I was beginning to lose my temper. "What's your real name?"

"I don't see why that would be important to you," he replied. "You'll have to make do with my sobriquet."

"Why are you following us?" Michael queried, stepping forward as if to menace the fae.

At least, a fae is what I was starting to think him to be.

His attitude of condescension and disinterest in our attempts to probe his origins were certainly fae-like.

"I'm not," he said. "I was just walking along the road, and you happened to be on it. Coincidence, happenstance, call it what you will. Please do not interrupt my journey."

"Where are you going?" I asked, baffled.

"Does it matter? I would have thought that that was obvious," he answered. "I am going to the market. I wish to barter for goods and then sell them for a profit."

"You are going to some market in central Zurich, predawn, and you happened to greet us here, by name."

"Do not get drawn in." It was Troy, finally with more to say. I had never heard his voice sound more tentative than it did in that moment.

"I know you." By then the thing's gnarly face and voice were clearly pointed in Troy's direction. "But do not act as if you know me. We've heard tell of you showing your face, and here I am seeing it with mine own eyes. It is not about me, it's about what I represent. My name isn't important," he said to us. "You may call me Henry."

"We don't give a damn for you," I said.

I was ready to charge forward and smash him across the face, but I didn't. There were forces at play which I did not believe any one of us understood.

The thing which identified itself as Henry vanished as suddenly as it appeared, although its stench lingered behind.

"Friend of yours?" Michael asked, turning to Troy.

Troy shook his head slowly. "We need not listen to him or heed his magic tricks."

"Like knowing my name?" I snarled.

"Exactly." After answering, Troy started to immediately walk into the building as if that could possibly be the end of it.

"Was that a fae?" Natasha questioned.

"I believe so," Troy said, pushing open the door to the lobby. "Or something like that. This realm is not his home."

I knew that Troy was right. Henry was clearly a creature of the woods, for his form was much like that of a traditional being haunted by a demonic existence—little more than a man-shaped child's nightmare, with everything about him being wrong, but only slightly so you would not be able to explain what was off in any meaningful sense.

Closing my eyes for a moment to try and picture Henry's face from just moments earlier, I could not be sure if the image in my mind's eye was that of our fresh encounter or a hazy memory nightmare resurfacing from some recent slumber.

Things became hazier with my growing fatigue as we rode the lift up to the flat, and I simply walked right into the nearest bedroom and collapsed.

"Evening, sleepyhead." With that greeting, Michael was the only one of my teammates to acknowledge me as I wandered into the living area after having slept some hours.

"What is happening?" I had to ask as I sat on the plush carpeted floor where Natasha, Troy, Michael, and Kieran were gathered, surrounded by notepads, pens, markers, and a map of Zurich serving as a centrepiece.

"I'll tell you what's happening." Troy sounded stressed, on the verge of angry. "More explosions, fires, a record-setting number of water mains bursting in the past week, more mysterious van accidents..."

"Kalgin, Alexander," Natasha interjected.

"In so many words, it would seem so," Troy conceded.

"You're always going to say that because one of them is after you." Michael placed his hand, in at least a half-joking way on Natasha's shoulder.

To her credit, Natasha literally shrugged him off.

"And what about Henry?" Michael pointed to Troy. "One of your friends, wasn't he?"

"Not friends," answered Troy, looking at the carpet. "But I recognized him as likely one of my own. But if it's demons terrorizing Zurich, or fae and their dark magic, all the incidents seem to be centered here, in this Friedhof park." Troy pointed to a green triangle on the map of Zurich.

"Actually, it's a cemetery," I noted. I recognized the map key symbol from where I stood.

"Really? That explains all the ghosts that have been sighted here lately," said Michael.

"Shut up," Natasha growled. It seemed like she may not have gotten much sleep since her nap on Troy's shoulder on the train. Usually she would be the first to laugh at one of Michael's jokes. "You do not even know what's been here lately. This is a place, I think it's clear now that this is the place of dark magic and demonic energy." She emphasized her point by tapping her finger against the map.

I knew Natasha was right, but I didn't expect her to be the one to say it. Still, I was glad she did, because none of the others suggested it. It seemed like they all wanted to go straight for the kill.

"We should split up and search the entire area," I suggested.

"We agreed that there was to be no splitting up," Natasha argued.

She looked straight up at me, the only one of the team standing, the odd man out, as I looked down at her sitting right next to Troy.

No splitting up, indeed.

"You're right." I conceded the point to Natasha as she was right, certainly, and my motivations for trying to split us all up may have been suspect at best.

And, besides, it looked as though my team had narrowed it down to a single location in Zurich. If the demons were coming through one spot, that was likely to be the portal. A portal that was a point on the pentagram, and one they would fight like hell, literally, to keep functional. This was something worth sacrificing not only my pride for, but all of us would need to give our all for, perhaps sacrificing everything.

"Let's go then," I said as I walked away from my team's little huddle on the floor and towards the door of the flat. The others followed and we descended down in the elevator.

The streets were empty, but if this was a point on the pentagram then there was one area that would be clogged with demonic activity. It would be a place where they feared not the light. We set off in that direction, sticking to the shadows as we moved through the streets of the city. The others were quiet and I knew exactly how they felt. "Is this the demon district?" Michael asked, showing his nervousness in his way. "Or the fae district?"

"It may be the latter, partially," Troy sighed.

We kept moving for several minutes until we reached our destination, a large graveyard. The street lights didn't reach there, or had fallen prey to one of the fires or outages, and the buildings were all close together, providing plenty of cover for anyone trying to lurk. That is what our first step was at least.

"Well, there's a few demon souls wandering about," I whispered as we snuck through the graveyard.

It is not likely that any of us were feeling great, exactly, since our arrival in Zurich. Yet the awful sensation which began to overtake me in that cemetery was almost unlike anything that I had felt previous in all my years. 'Almost' because there was one exception: just before we had fallen through the magic portal in Paris. This time, there was that deathly aura which started to surround everything around us, including the gravestones. There was also the distinct feeling that something was watching us.

The deathly quiet which had seemed to envelope Switzerland's largest city since we had been there was abruptly shattered by an aural blanket of shrill panic, a swell of terrified screaming surrounding us as a red fog came pouring out of the portal, engulfing the cemetery.

We had been spotted.

"Where are you running to?" a familiar voice scratched through the thick sounds of terror. Whether we were running or not, which we were not, seemed to make no difference to it. I could tell, and could smell, that it was that Henry thing again. His long, loping gait easily kept pace with me as he walked alongside, and I didn't dare tear my eyes away from him to see if the others were holding their own against the demons that must surely be swarming them.

"Why are you running, little bird? Why not embrace your fate?" he asked in that annoyingly coy voice of his.

"Shut up, you!" Troy yelled at the Henry-thing, to which he responded by staring at him, his eyes narrowing.

For the first time, I caught sight of an actual one of these portals created as part of the apocalyptic ritual. The ground was split wide open, like the wound of some great beast, and an unearthly blue light emanated out of it. I was reminded of the first time I walked through the gates of Hell, and the sickly radiance that leached out from within.

I was so distracted by the terrible sight and the memory it brought back that I forgot to pay attention to my assailants— and there were myriad assailants. Countless small demonic monsters. I was brought back to reality by something sharp sinking into my side. I spun on the thing, lashing out and tearing it away with a blow, but more of them were already swarming me.

"Do something with that nuclear angel shit you have!" I heard Michael yell, imploring Natasha to summon her full power. Indeed, it seemed as though the plague of small to medium-sized demons were descending relentlessly upon all of us as shrieking, terrified human souls flew past us and into the portal.

"I'm trying," Natasha said, so weighed down by a cloud of insect-like monsters attacking her that she could barely move. "I'm trying to summon a full blast. It's dangerous."

"Do you want to get out of here alive or not?" I heard him roar. "This is your last chance!"

"I-I am sorry if this ends up hurting any of you...or worse," she said with an obvious quiver in her voice. "Forgive me."

Immediately after those words from Natasha a dazzlingly brilliant flash of white light overtook the world around us. This was nothing like the lesser fireballs Natasha had summoned during our previous run-in with the demons. This was the full power of heaven unleashed upon the cemetery and all the beings in it.

There was a balmy heat I could feel with the blinding light, singing the hairs on my skin.

As the flash subsided and my vision returned to normal, I could not help but be shocked by the scene before me. There was a sooty, black semicircle of burnt earth emanating from Natasha, and it looked as though the worst of the blast had just missed where I had stood. There were no demons remaining, none, only my teammates, all of us dazed, and a small group of what looked like fairies gathered by the portal. Natasha had managed to bowl over with the force of her own blast, and she looked to be barely holding onto consciousness as she had fallen backwards into Troy's arms.

We all rushed over to her.

"That was the big one," Natasha managed to say before coughing violently.

"We need your help!" Troy shouted at the gathered fairies, his voice quivering wildly with desperation. "We might need your magic! She might need it."

"What about your own magic, princey?" To my shock, the Henry-thing was still there, standing in the crowd.

"I...I don't have it in me right now." I had never seen Troy sob before, but he seemed to be right on the verge as Natasha sunk lower to the ground and he held her as tightly as he could.

"We are not here to serve you," a fae answered. The fae appeared as a young man, not unlike Troy. "That is no longer our duty. Not since time immemorial."

Grasping Natasha in his arms, there was a dawning of realization in Troy's eyes.

"You're here to actively help...not us, but..."

"The king does not want us to help you," the Henry-thing sneered.

"They're with the demons," Troy muttered softly before lifting Natasha off the ground entirely.

"You thought we would not be your enemies, on your enemy's side? You thought the past just never existed?" the Henry-thing asked in a sing-song voice. "That seems unlikely."

"Fuck you!" Those words coming from Troy's mouth were enough to send another kind of shockwave through me and the rest of the team. "There's no time for this, we need to get her to safety."

Troy turned around and started to carry Natasha, now unconscious, away from the scene.

9

CHAPTER NINE A TOWN CALLED SINS

Natasha

Natasha, please, you are almost here, I can feel it. Please come back to me, to us.

My head was pounding, my throat was as dry as it had ever been, my stomach felt like a hollow, ravenous void as it gurgled fiercely for a second or two.

And those words sounded as if they were being beamed in from some alien radio station across the galaxy, the sound hollow and tinny, caught somewhere between the ghostly remembrance of some long-ago conversation and the final stirrings of some an old, damaged telephone receiver attempting to relay a few more words from a friend before it died completely.

What were you thinking, Natasha?

There were a few more words, coming in much more clearly. Almost surreally vivid, in fact, like those few seconds of sound from a television jolting you awake just as you were about to drift off.

You put yourself at so much danger. And now... why?

There was the sensation of my own hand, the butt of my palm, rubbing some dull ache just off my right temple.

The sensation of my hand, the sound of the voice—which I slowly recognized as Troy's—started to feel real. And I tried to remember what was real, and what I could remember at all, if anything.

I remembered the brilliance, the pure light of everything within myself I could summon made outward.

It was as if the entire scope of my existence and my soul and all of my inner colours condensed and concentrated in a section of a cemetery, an area smaller than a rugby pitch, the entire universe of my life pushed out and made out in and the open and as plain as day.

What were you thinking, *Natasha?*

"Michael asked me to," I breathed quietly, answering before I even knew where I was.

"Since when should any of us listen to Michael?"

Troy's response sounded a bit put off, but as I opened my eyes to see him looking down at me, there was a distinct smile on his lips.

"You know what? I don't care. You are awake now. I was so worried about you."

I tried to sit up, but found myself coughing and aching a bit all over.

"Here," said Troy, handing me a glass of water he had at the ready. Who knew how long he had been waiting for me, perhaps even holding the glass as he spoke to me, watching for signs of my awakening.

As I took my first sip, I felt Troy's hand laying ever so gently on my hair, just to where it hung over my left cheek. I assumed Troy was only trying to help wake me up and bring me back into reality through the sensation of a light touch, and it was working at that. Troy moved his hand from my hair to my face, and he cupped my chin for a flash of a second before letting go. My headache seemed to ease up a bit.

"Thank you," I said, smiling.

"You seemed to be able to handle your powers just fine days ago." Troy was back at it, acting like a concerned teacher or something. "But you went too far with it, did you not? Promise me you will be more careful."

"Where are we?" I asked before taking another sip of the warm tap water.

"An abandoned home. Just outside Zurich, in this town called Sins, I think."

I almost did a genuine spit-take, coughing up some water when I heard that.

"Is it really called Sins?"

Troy's hands held me gingerly by stomach and the small of my back.

"Careful, Natasha. And yes, it is called that. And really, it's not that funny. At least, I'm not sure why it would be."

"I beg to differ." After taking another gulp of water I noticed my headache was nearly gone and overall I had begun to feel much, much better. "How long have I been out?"

"Four days," replied Troy. "The team and I recovered you and brought you here after you fell. You nearly died, I thought. Why did you seem fine after using your powers so recently? You should have known there would be such a degree of difference going full blast like that."

I looked around the dark room lit only by a candle and the twilight coming through a slender window adjacent to the head of the cot where I lay.

"I guess we couldn't go back to the Zurich flat, with that Henry bloke and all that." I rubbed away the last nagging bits of subtle pain around my forehead.

"Correct. It was not just Henry, but, well, the annoying crowd who would pester us there. But really, Natasha, do you know why employing your powers affected you to such a degree this time?"

"I've grown accustomed to a certain degree of usage, as you know." I gulped down the rest of my water. "About the power, I mean. But I do not dare draw deeply from that reservoir. Usually, I just skim the top of it."

Troy moved closer to me, his eyes remaining doggedly full of concern. "You say you don't dare draw your full power. But you did. You put yourself in danger, Natasha!"

"It was needed." The reason I found myself smiling at Troy, just like the reason he seemed so doting and concerned, was a mystery. "Why do you care so much?"

His fingertips brushed against my wrist, lightly but with a slow pace and subtle friction with implied urgency.

"Because," he said, "we spend so much time together. I don't want you to get hurt. You mean a lot to me."

The look in Troy's eyes, it was hard to describe. And it only inspired more questions, questions I did not bother to ask because, for whatever reason, I was enjoying it. Especially as he drew himself even closer.

The kiss, Troy's kiss, came so suddenly and deeply that I had no time to consider what even that meant, what anything meant, nor did I care. His lips were warm and comforting against mine. I felt like all the weariness of the world was just melting away with each languid movement of our lips.

As we both brought our bodies closer to each other, with Troy practically climbing onto the cot with me, things started to take a turn for the, shall we say, feral. His hands started wandering a bit, second currents of electric warmth through me as they slid between my back and the firm mattress. My own hands mimicked Troy's, sliding up and down the rocky musculature of his back. Feeling Troy breathing deeply, at an increasing speed against my hands, I found the energy to pull him down towards me, even closer, feeling the need for his closeness more and more there nearer he got to me and the more stiffly and powerfully our lips pressed into each other.

The tip of my tongue wandered into Troy's mouth first, and as he only helped me closer and moved his lips against mine with more hungry ferocity, I slid my tongue in more, starting to feel almost feverish with desire as I felt his weight beginning to press on top of me.

When Troy's tongue gripped my own, that mild fever of desire blossomed into the stirrings of a deep, primal, aching hunger. It was the sort of famishment that I had not felt in a long time. So long, I could not remember, but I cared only for bringing my awakening flower of feral desire to fruition in a way that I felt in my bones could only happen with Troy.

I let out a quiet moan as my tongue fought with his, before feeling him starting to push me down against the cot.

When I felt the cottony softness of my pillow under my head, I felt my hands finding their determined way up to Troy's muscular chest. It was like my hands had a mind of their own, attracted to the statuesque beauty of his muscle tone that they slid up to his pecs magnetically and the feelings of Troy's rock hard body breathing under my palms and fingers almost came as a surprise.

It felt so wild, so raw, so not what I would ever expect with Troy. So not what I had ever experienced with anyone, not even Alexander.

My hand slowly traced the planes of his pectorals before greedily slipping down to his abdominals and taking in every wonderful nuance. Our lips never broke apart. I felt drunk on our very own supply of oxygen. It could have been, should have been, the exact wrong time for any of this, but it only made me feel more alive.

All I wanted to do was tell him not to stop, to let this slow simmer turn into a full on sizzle until we were both well-done, when the door burst open and we jumped back from each other just as quickly. I'd completely forgotten about being tired.

"Well, well, well." Of course it was Michael who just had to comment first.

And of course, I could hear the smirk in his voice before I could see it, but I did see it, and him, and Kieran, and Alexander, all watching us from just the other side of the door.

"Did not any one of you ever learn how to knock?" Troy demanded.

"The door was closed, but not locked," Michael retorted.

"How long have you all been standing there?" I asked, a little too late to still be considered coy, I guessed.

"Long enough," replied Michael with a shit-eating grin. "You two are more passionate than the congregation's choir! I really hope it sounds better when you're actually having sex."

Of course he had to say something like that.

I could have very well told Michael that Troy and I had never had sex, but instead of giving him the satisfaction I only looked down while feeling my cheeks flush brightly.

Even Kieran was so damn amused he let out, get this, a wolf-whistle.

The boys all thought it was funny, and to be fair, I probably would've too if I wasn't the main joke. Not your fault, I told myself. It really isn't your fault, but you're going to have to do something about it.

"Boys," I said as I went into the room towards them.

This caused all of them to stop laughing, though they knew what was coming next.

Well, they all stopped laughing—except Alexander, who I then realized was not laughing at all. He was staring out the window, an odd sort of unfocused angst in his eyes.

"Is everything okay?" I asked him.

His response was no response. He just continued to stare out the tiny window as if he were deaf.

"Hey!" I shouted at him, and he finally turned towards me.

"I was just...are you okay? We were all worried."

"I am fine now, clearly," I stated, with my arms crossed.

There was very little light coming through the window, as it appeared to be the gloaming—past dusk and before the darkness of nighttime fully set in. The reason I noted these things was that I could not blame the unusual pallor of Alexander's complexion on the dim lighting. I had never seen him look so pale, and for obvious reasons that was saying something. Instead of playing the whole 'are you okay' card that him and Troy seemed suddenly obsessed with playing with me, especially as I had already asked him once, I decided to just leave it alone.

"Any word from Director Hask?" I asked nobody in particular.

"Yes," Alexander answered, having gone back to staring out the window. "He wants us to report to the congregation's Rome headquarters where he's working currently."

"There's the other reported portal there," Kieran then reminded everybody. "It might be a better place to start looking for leads."

"Well then, I guess we had better get going, hm? After you lot waited for me for, how long was I out for again?"

"Four days," Michael said, alarming me a bit, though I think I hid that well.

"Too much time lost," I remarked. "But on the bright side, that means more time for me to rest and get ready for the next hunt."

"The less time you spend asleep, the better," Alexander teased. It may have very well been my imagination, or my brain insisting on playing tricks after a few days of unplanned sleep, but the usual, marginally less pale colour appeared to be making a reappearance on Alexander's face as well.

"Truer words have never been spoken," I replied, grinning at Alexander and doing my best to encourage him to climb out of whatever crisis his vampire emotions could possibly be dragging him through.

There was work to be done, after all, and as a way of signalling my readiness I looked at the others expectantly. They all continued just to stare, either at me or the ground, waiting for me to take the reins as I had been doing more and more often.

So, taking the reins is exactly what I did.

"Well? We going or what? I'm not getting any younger, you know."

10

ENTRY OF THE GLADIATORS

Troy

In hundreds of years of existence, I had seen fewer things more amazing than the swiftness of Natasha's recovery.

As for me, my recovery had been less impressive. Granted, I only did spend a couple of minutes attempting to keep the demons at bay outside the portal, but after witnessing it... I didn't know why I was surprised. I just remained a bit painful and stiff.

"Emilio will update us in person?" Natasha asked, having more energy than us all as she walked ahead of us through a house she knew nothing of and towards the front door.

"Yes, Hask will be waiting," replied Kieran, tapping away at his phone. "And my phone is almost dead by now."

"So, how are we getting there?" I asked, doing my best to keep up with Natasha, Michael, and Kieran.

Alexander was the only team member who was trailing behind me as we hurried towards the door.

"Um, I think Hask messaged me about that just before my

screen went blank." Kieran had stopped suddenly, staring at his now powerless phone. "But, I must have read it wrong."

"What did it say?" I asked.

"It said we're taking a helicopter," he replied.

"Damn it," Natasha cursed under her breath. "I was hoping for a few more hours to relax. I didn't get the chance to enjoy my time off, not being awake for it and all."

"We don't have a choice, though," said Alexander. "I mean, how long would it take us to drive there?"

"He's right," said Michael.

As if waiting for its queue, we heard the sound of a helicopter engine whirring as it landed somewhere just outside the front door.

"Guess I read that message right after all," marvelled Kieran.

"Come on, the copter's idling outside and that fuel is not cheap," Natasha implored us while opening the front door. The sky was darkening as the sun set and we saw our ride, a black helicopter marked with a small facsimile of the congregation's insignia painted on it in white. The aircraft was congregation property, apparently, although it was clearly designed to avoid attracting much attention. It was essentially unmarked. The team ducked their heads to avoid the still spinning propeller and made their way towards the helicopter's cabin while I just stood there, feeling the strange tingling feeling.

It was not unlike what I often felt when something extraordinary was happening. It was a subtle feeling that could accompany excitement, but I knew it also could mean I needed to be on guard, that I was sensing something unusual occurring. I felt the need to take a quick look around the empty field and the nearby dense patch of trees, but nothing I could see was out of the ordinary. There was just a peculiar feeling I had in my gut, and my heart which seemed to be going much faster than was typical.

"Come on, Troy, time is wasting away!" Kieran shouted, slipping into his more assertive, schedule-keeping mode.

Or, perhaps I had imagined it, as I saw nothing but darkness coming from the wood as I ran to board the copter.

"Oh for...Troy! Stop your mournful dawdling and climb aboard the helicopter this instant!"

I clambered inside.

We were soon in the air. The view of the countryside was quite pleasant, if you ignored the reason for our journey. We were soon over the Adriatic Sea, which was much darker than the sky, making its presence known only when we flew over tiny islands.

"This is an interesting route we are taking," I remarked.

"Better to fly mostly over water," Alexander answered automatically, thumbing through some old, leather-bound volume he had of some book or other.

Usually it was the other way around when traveling by air, but I could only imagine that there was some sort of congregation agreement in flight plans in Italian airspace. Likely for the safety of all involved.

Soon we were over land again, crossing over the east coast of Italy, somewhere around Pescara on the way to the congregation's growing facilities in Rome.

As we approached the city and the bright lights beneath us became brighter and denser, I noticed Alexander switch from briefly looking out the window to sticking his nose back into whatever book he was reading—likely to avoid seeing any glimpse of Vatican City, which for him must have been a dreadful sight indeed.

As the helicopter lowered itself gradually somewhere on the outskirts of Rome proper, I saw what must have been the command centre for the congregation. It certainly looked like it belonged to some sort of military or national security force rather than something like the congregation.

"We're landing at our secondary airport, just outside of

the city," Alexander explained when he saw me looking out the window. "From here, Hask should have a car to take us to the portal here in Rome. Where it is in the city."

"Hopefully he will know where that is, too," Natasha remarked quietly.

Upon landing, I saw that this airport was actually a good deal larger than what I expected for something neighbouring the congregation in Rome. The helicopter was soon off-loaded onto a large tarmac with dozens of other helicopters and small private planes. No sooner had our helicopter landed than it was taken away to some hangar to make room for the next arrival. From there, we walked onto the taxiway to see a large, black American SUV of some sort pull to a stop right in our path.

"He's sending Hummers for us now," Natasha sighed, slightly annoyed for some reason. The SUV in question had heavily tinted windows, so you couldn't see who was inside. The moment we stepped onto the taxiway, however, all doors unlocked and the rear passenger door opened slightly.

"Is it weird that I'm getting into a car with someone who could be anyone inside?" I asked nervously.

"Just get in," Natasha said. "Cars are a lot harder to rig to kill you than planes or even helicopters."

"Maybe for you," I grumbled, climbing in.

The interior looked pretty posh, and smelled new. The moment I sat down, the door shut behind me and the car pulled away from the tarmac even before Natasha got inside. Whoever was driving didn't turn to look at us, but had to have known we were sitting in the back.

"Hask has good taste in cars," Natasha said, sliding over to make room for me. The car was big enough that we could sit facing each other in the back, even with our seat belts on. "He doesn't like to splurge on himself, but he knows how to treat others."

"He can't be making that much money as a director," I

said, leaning against the armrest as we rode smoothly along the roadway circling outer Rome.

"So this car alone is a splurge," a faint yet oddly familiar voice commented from behind the closed screen which separated us from the driver's seat.

Natasha frowned. "How much do you think a congregation director makes?"

I shrugged. "Twenty grand? Hundred thousand quid? Something like that."

"Try again," the voice said. It was a woman's voice, I realised, as faint and gruff as it sounded.

"One million?" Natasha laughed. "Wait...Mrs. Beatrice?"

"Yes. And higher," Mrs. Beatrice said, lowering the screen to reveal that she was, indeed, Director Hask's receptionist whom we all knew and loved. "Try again."

"Five million?" I tried.

"Higher," Beatrice said.

"Twenty million?" Alexander nearly had a trace of laughter in his voice as he entered his own contribution to the exchange.

"And is this euro or quid?" Kieran asked, joining in on the fun in the only way he knew how.

"Does it matter at that point? And also, higher," Beatrice said, sounding annoyed.

"A hundred million pounds?" Natasha asked.

The car stopped, and she popped the screen back up again. "Well, we're here. I know at least one of you boys is readying to open the door for me and then you can head inside."

I felt myself smiling lightly, looking out at the congregation's Rome headquarters.

The building was massive, easily the size of a castle from the outside. Large and looming, dark stone blocks making up its construction. My smile nearly turned into a laugh when I noticed the door to the SUV's cabin opening on its own.

"You don't need our help, these doors open on their own." Natasha was echoing my thoughts, although she sounded a bit more irritated. "And are you not coming inside with us?"

"I guess not now," Mrs. Beatrice shot back at Natasha in that vague way of hers. "You're all adults, you can find your way around."

None of us could have argued with that logic if we had wanted.

Walking into the refurbished office and academic building where Hask was working, it did indeed look empty, with fluorescent lights humming over empty hallways. Natasha silently led us to Hask's clearly marked office on the first floor.

For the first time in hours I saw Natasha let her lips relax a bit and form into something akin to a smile as she knocked on the office door.

"It's open!" Hask's voice informed us, and Natasha smiled warmly as she led us into the office.

"Hey, Emilio," she greeted him, seeing him sitting behind his desk, the glow of a computer screen illuminating his face.

Hask, who I last remember as being in his mid-fifties but looking like he was in his late thirties, looked up at us, smiling as he recognised each of us.

"Ah, Natasha, it's good to see you. You've grown since the last time I saw you."

"Very funny," Natasha said, her smile dropping just slightly. "We just wanted to stop by to see you while we could."

"I understand," he said. "I know this must be not the kind of assignment you signed up for, or have prepared for but you have to realise that this world is at stake, and there will be sacrifices that need to be made if we are to prevent the destruction of everything."

"We know," Natasha said, looking at us. "We're ready to do our duty, aren't we, team?"

We all nodded, with Michael just barely able to hold in a chuckle in response to Natasha's earnest pep talk.

"Very well," Hask said. "Now let's get you to the portal; you're already very late for it."

"Where, pray tell, is this portal?" asked Alexander.

"Oh, this little place you may have heard of by Palatine Hill. But, before I get to that, I've got a gift, of sorts, for Natasha."

"What is this you're talking about?" Natasha raised an eyebrow quizzically at the director.

"This is about your sword," said Hask, handing Natasha what appeared to be an old scroll of near-crumbling parchment paper.

Natasha regarded the scroll in her hand with a growing bemusement. "What does this have to do with my sword?"

"You should be getting better at figuring these things out by now." Hask was outright grinning—watching him as he regarded Natasha and her sour confusion at the piece of parchment, I could not recall ever seeing the director act so cheeky. "And I know you've always been much cleverer than most."

Natasha's bewilderment only seemed to grow as she held the scroll.

"Those words are not as inspiring as I'm sure they sounded in your head."

Before hearing Natasha's response, I would not have thought it possible to bring the entire motley crew gathered in the director's office to laughter. Natasha herself seemed tickled by her own response, wearing a coy smirk as the rest of us chortled loudly.

"Here's a hint my dear: what you hold in your hand is nothing without your own special abilities. Without them, it really is just a roll of parchment."

"And this is supposed to be a complement to my sword?" Natasha held the scroll up to examine it better, revealing it to look pale and translucent in the overhead lighting. "Like a shield or something."

"I knew you'd get it quickly." Hask nodded, his grin having settled into a soft, subtle smile.

"And this will protect me from what exactly? A bullet? A...claw?"

Hask cleared his throat. "From the creatures you'll face on this mission, not necessarily. But it's a start."

Natasha growled a bit, which for some odd reason bright a touch of blushing to my cheeks.

"I'm a bit tired now, but..."

There was a small flash of light, nothing from what we had seen from her in our last battle or any battle before that. It was more akin to a camera flash, or an incandescent light bulb just before burning out. However, immediately after the flash had cleared, Natasha no longer had a scroll in her hand, but was decked out in a sleek, comfortable, yet formidable looking version of the armour a Roman centurion may have worn marching into the British Isles.

"How do I look?" she asked, doing a slow turn for all of us to see.

I did not know how to respond at first, but then Michael chuckled and said "Like Coco Chanel's interpretation of the Praetorian Guard."

"Like *what?*" Natasha huffed, showing much more annoyance than sincere curiosity.

"A...never mind," Michael laughed.

I did not laugh.

I stared at the woman before me in shock and awe.

I never thought I would see such a...such a vision.

She was like an angel, no scratch that, she WAS an angel. Even through my stress and exhaustion, I was compelled to spend a wondrous moment taking it all in. I was glad that I did.

Natasha's eyes were a verdant shade of emerald which

struck me to my core. Her skin, even though none of us had been able to properly care for ourselves in days, was pure, pale, and flawless. Her body was that of a goddess's, a glimpse of its cursive beauty enough to send even the dead into waves of passionate heat. Her face was of a beauty which was not classical, only because it transcended space and then. And she stood there, cloaked in a blood red robe with golden lining, a silver sword strapped to her side.

Her light, golden hair was stunning even when was pulled back into a ponytail, with loose ringlets falling over her forehead, stopping just short of her large, round, cherubic eyes. Those eyes of hers lit an especially large spark within me as I looked at her under the guise of seeing her magical armour. Her eyes were round indeed but with an upturn which gave them the hint of an intoxicating almond shape, and the brightness of their colour and the power of their gaze pierced through me. Her armour fit perfectly on her slender yet muscular frame. Even while fatigued and rumpled as the rest of us, she still looked more beautiful than any being of any kind I had seen.

And even though she was silent standing there, as I took in her beauty sense memories of her melodic and enchanting voice, her angelic voice, played around with me and struck up sparks of desire throughout my mind and soul.

"Where is this portal again?" Alexander's question broke my enchanted reverie, which was alright as we all needed to be in top shape.

"Well, about that, my gladiators," Hask began.

"Gladiators?" I interrupted.

"Yes, gladiators. You are all warriors, fighters, chevaliers and heroes in our great fight," Hask tried to explain.

"Wait a second," I raised my hand as if I were back in class in my earlier days at the congregation.

"Wait a second, indeed," Alexander hissed. "I am no gladiator, sent to fight and die for others' amusement in the Circus Maximus. Or the damned Colosseum!"

"Right," replied Hask, briskly to the door behind his desk. "Except for the Colosseum part, because that is where the demons have their portal here in Rome."

Hask opened the door just enough to reach out and retrieve a very dear looking beige suit jacket. While I knew the door led to a closet of sorts, I realised I had no idea how large that closet was. I deduced it could not have been very sizable for him to just reach in like that.

Hask slipped the jacket on over his shirt and vest. He buttoned a single button, clearly in the starting stages of preparing for something.

"Let me get this straight," I began, trying to maintain the director's focus as well as my own. "The demons have chosen locations for the pentagram ritual not only in the midst of the largest cities in their countries, but in this instance literally in the dead centre of one of the most populated cities on Earth?"

"Exactly! This is where the souls are concentrated." Hask swiftly smoothed and straightened his suit before reaching back towards the closet door.

"Now that Natasha has her armour, let's get you boys suited up, shall we?"

"But what about the police?" Kieran queried in an urgent manner which made clear he'd held in the question as long he could. "Or the authorities here in Rome. This is one of the country's biggest landmarks."

"The police..." Hask shook his head. "Things are getting just as bad here as they are anywhere, the police can no longer be bothered with some old ruins. Plus, when you get there, you will see why every human is scared shitless of going within a ten kilometre radius."

Hask pushed the door open completely, revealing not a

closet but a vast, well-lit storage space easily twice as large as the office where we stood.

My teammates and I followed the director into the expansive space. The air was noticeably chillier there, and there were various garments and a few weapons hung on the walls.

However, most immediately noticeable were the four sets of armour prominently displayed on limbless mannequins. The armour sets vaguely resembled Natasha's, albeit far less stylish.

"The helicopter retrieving you lot gave me ample opportunity to dig out these ancient battle-suit replicas I've been saving for such an occasion. I also had them to take them out a bit."

There was clearly one for each of us, and while I didn't question anything else about this plan, I wondered how Hask knew our correct sizes.

"Try them on," said Hask. "I prepared them so you wouldn't have to waste time fetching your regular gear. And also so you boys would not feel left out after Natasha got her shield up."

Alexander, Kieran, Michael, and I all took the hint about timing and with no further delay we all went to gearing up in the provided equipment, each of us choosing the suit which seemed to be roughly our size.

The armour was heavier than it looked, but after I managed to squeeze into mine it felt secure and, from what I could sense, aerodynamic.

"Humans were very small two thousand years ago," Michael gasped, having some problems with his armour until he shifted into a shorter version of himself. "Phew. That is much better."

Turning to face him briefly, I noticed that Michael had also taken the opportunity to shift his face into that of Russel Crowe's.

"I know it's not quite as handsome as my usual face," he shrugged, "but he got an Oscar for it."

"Hell's bells," I commented, not really knowing what else to say. "That is really something."

"Give it a rest," added Natasha. I could tell she was rolling her eyes by the annoyance in her voice.

Hask led us out to the main driveway—I noted that it did feel surprisingly comfortable at least, walking in the armour —and drove us himself in a giant black SUV identical to the one which had taken us there from the airport.

Even as it approached the witching hour, the streets of Rome were packed with vehicles, jamming narrow motor-ways and honking endlessly. Things did begin to get considerably less crowded as we penetrated the heart of central Rome and got closer to the Colosseum.

There was a pale, blue light emanating from nearly every surface which seemed to get stronger the closer we got. When I spotted the Colosseum itself, it was like something out of *Ghostbusters*. Even with the lights on the outside, it was lit up from the inside like a Christmas tree. Hask pulled over to the side of the road, where we could get a better view of what was going on.

"It looks like the circus is in town." I was starting to see the value in sarcasm more and more as I found myself using it with increasing frequency. The streets were practically empty save for the occasional car trying to edge its way past us.

"That's no circus," said Hask gravely. "That's a feeding frenzy."

11

AMPHITHEATRE OF THE COLOSSUS

Natasha

"*L*et's get this over with," I said, not knowing what to expect, except that it was yet another stop on the journey, and none of us had the foggiest as to how the journey would end—or when it would end, that was.

"You got it," said Michael, climbing through the open door of the car and steered towards the ancient stadium, now bathed in some ungodly glow.

"This could be the end of it," I whispered.

After Michael, the rest of the team piled out of the car. We were parked on the side of one of the many streets laid out in a cramped fashion around the area. Across from us stood the Colosseum, lit up in a multi-coloured hue, although the colour tones were all dull and dim. The immensity of the demonic aura over the ancient stadium juxtaposed with the paleness of the colours made for a deeply disquieting contrast. There were no cars there; the road was empty save for a few bits of debris from whatever mayhem had occurred in recent days.

I looked around and was alarmed at what I saw. While we

were piling out of the car, I saw that there were no people on the streets. Not a single person. It was like the entire population had dropped what they were doing and just… left.

"What the hell happened here?" said Michael, echoing my thoughts.

I looked up at the sky. Through the sparse clouds, I could see a full moon lighting up the scene with an eerie glow.

"It's the full moon, tonight," I said.

"Not quite," answered Kieran as he caught up with us on the way to the Colosseum's entrance. "Believe me, it's in my best interest to keep on top of these things."

As if on cue, there was a howl from far off in the city. It could have been a dog, or a wolf stalking the streets of Rome in the dead of night for whatever reason, or just a distraction somehow created by the demons in order to discourage and disorient.

"Let's just get inside," said Alexander.

The gate in front of us opened distressingly on its own as we approached it. It was a magnificent structure, worthy of an empire founded by ancient warrior-kings, but right now, all I could see was an entrance to a slaughterhouse. I saw a lion's head made out of wrought iron on one side of the gate.

The others could not see what I was seeing. Michael, the first one in, did not even bother to look at the gate as he passed through. He disappeared from my view immediately after entering the Colosseum.

Immediately upon entering I could see the portal. It was large with a blackened aura around its changing colours, hovering in mid-air without the aid of any discernible machinery. The symbols on it seemed to be transforming themselves all the time, from different alphabets to bizarre mathematical symbols, never resting long enough for me to even begin to read them.

There was an intermittent red glow also emanating from

it, casting an unsettling light on the area. Occasionally people were sucked into it by an unseen force.

How those poor souls had ended up there I would likely never know, but as I took in the sight of the empty stands flanking the portal, I could not help but think of the Christians and the other captives forced to live out terrifying, life-threatening ordeals in front of horrifyingly delighted crowds in that very stadium.

Of course, if I were correct about the nature of this portal, then those people had most likely been transported straight into hell.

As soon as I had that thought, a bright flash of lightning erupted from the portal and struck the ground just in front of where my teammates had just entered. A great roar of thunder accompanied it, ensnaring every fibre of my perception in its vibrations. I found myself on my knees clutching my ears in pain.

There was another flash, and another roar, but this time it struck somewhere in the stands next to where I was on the Colosseum floor. Pushing myself back up to my feet, I heard an awful scream that was abruptly cut off.

Ripping my magic feather from my side, ready to activate it into sword form, I whirled around to see the charred figure of a man collapse and roll down a nearby set concrete steps, landing right in front of my feet.

"Damn it!" I heard Alexander shout. "It's some kind of lightning portal! They have it set up as a trap to protect itself. Be careful!"

Focusing my vision, hoping I could conjure some angelic energy to my vision in order to pierce the darkness and notice any oncoming attacks, I turned back towards the portal. Almost as if in response to my action, another bolt of lightning appeared there. As it struck a bit farther away this time, I was able to see a figure standing at the edge of the portal just before I was hit by a deafening clap of thunder.

The strike of lightning threw me back several feet, my body tingling and vision blurring. The ringing in my ears was so bad that I could no longer hear the sounds of the battle from inside the Colosseum. Groaning, I picked myself up, shaking my head as to get my bearings, only to catch the sight of Alexander circling through the air before my eyes, landing with an awful thud somewhere on the edge of my peripheral vision.

"Damn it, Kieran!" I heard Alexander swear through the racket of lightning crashes from the portal. "I was distracting it for you!"

"I've got problems of my own here," I heard Kieran yell before his voice fell into a literal growl.

As my vision and hearing recovered further from the demonic lighting strike, I could make out Kieran grappling with a shadowy figure. Literally, a shadow figure. It was humanoid in shape, composed of seemingly pure darkness, and those shadow monsters were running roughshod over the entire Colosseum as bright blue, green, and turquoise bursts of lightning continued to burst forth from the portal with horrible crashes and bangs.

If all of that were not horrid enough, I realized I was no longer holding my magic feather, which meant I had no sword.

"Really? This now?" I groused while scanning the section of Colosseum floor around me. "I can't be left without a weapon right now!"

My shout was overtaken by Kieran's grunts and snarls, as several of the shadow demons approached him from all directions and his hands flew in every direction as he did his best to fight them off.

One of the shadow things was, unsurprisingly, trying to take a run at me as I had probably drawn attention to myself with my outburst.

Before it could get to me Troy side-lined it with a tackle,

only for another of the shadow monsters to try to wrap its arms around my torso, having snuck up from the side.

I lifted my arms up above my head and the demon was not able to get a grip on me through my armour. I then proceeded to drop my weight and fall back, landing the demon on its back in a heap. I quickly regained my footing and drove my heel into its dumb, shadowy face, making cracks of grey and brown appear across its head as it screamed out before falling silent.

The entire time this was happening I was briefly distracted by how Troy fought off the other shadow being with his bare hands. He, like from what I saw of Kieran, was just holding it together, and there were more shadows swarming in his direction.

And I could not even catch sight of where Alexander and Kieran were, or how they were faring, but it could not have been good.

"Oh, fuck it," I said as a shadow demon tried grabbing my neck from behind. "Time to go all out."

I body slammed that demon to the ground in front of me. I was still in a crouched position as I quickly looked for where my sword had fallen. Seeing it some distance away, near the pile of dead demons, I knew that I would not have enough time to get to it before the demons managed to attack me again.

"Fuck!" I cried out in frustration and, without looking, I channelled all of that moment's frustrated energy—which was indeed no small amount—into the palm of my hand.

The palm blast that I released instantly scorched through the cluster of demons closest to me, leaving a trail of burnt ash in its wake. The searing comet of light emanating from the blast kept hurtling forward until it burned straight through the demons Troy was striving to fight off and then proceeded to zoom at a relentless velocity until finally it hit a row of lower stands across the Colosseum, sending that section of the stadium into a small tremor before the energy dissipated into the cool night air.

As the blast had revealed where my feather was, not far from the Colosseum entrance, I quickly scrambled to my feet and ran over to where it was. Picking it up, for the first time I channelled some of my own energy while activating it. After a monumental bright blue flame burst forth the blade which appeared was larger and sharper than it had ever been before, glistening in the moonlight.

I turned around and saw that the battle was still not yet won, but I knew that it could be. The blade was gigantic and heavy, more like a claymore than a rapier, but the weight gave it power.

I zipped as fast as my feet were carrying me to where the boys were struggling against the demons. For the first time since we had entered the Colosseum I could see all four of them, and it seemed as though the demons had them somehow herded together whether my teammates had realised it or not. Only Kieran and Alexander were directly facing me as I ran towards them, and when they spotted me their eyes went wide with horror.

"Natasha! What are you doing? Put that away, it's too heavy and it will do more harm than good!" Michael screamed at me. I ignored him and ran forward with the sword raised. I let out a shrill, ferocious battle cry as I ran into the heart of the action, and before I knew it, I was right in the centre a dense cluster of shadowy demons.

With all of the might, strength, power, and potency I could muster, I swung the sword.

The sword became a circular, silvery blur as I reeled it around me savagely, catching all the demons around me in its swing. The ones closest to me fell down instantly, as their once relentlessly murky and opaque forms showed hairline cracks of ochre and grey as they fell.

As I continued to swing, the others quickly stepped back to avoid the path of the blade.

"Come get some, shadow bitches!" I cried out.

The rest of the demons seemed to hesitate for a moment as the shadow monsters seemed to be communicating with each other that this one be cray.

And, if that was indeed what they were thinking, then they would certainly be correct about that.

"I will show you the light of the world, *motherfuckers!*" With that, a supernova of a fireball detonated from within me, bathing the entire Colosseum in what seemed like the light of day, at least for a few seconds.

The heat and light would have been enough to turn anyone to ash, but I shielded my eyes with my hand for a moment as the demons around me fried and fell off of me.

When I opened my eyes again, the sword was glowing brightly, almost too bright to look at.

I swung it wildly, cutting down any demon that came near me.

Soon, only a few stragglers remained.

"Ah!" I heard a voice, likely one of the souls freed from the now powerless portal, shout from behind me.

Spinning around, I could see that for this first time my angelic blast had created, for lack of a better term, a mushroom cloud. A rising fireball of pure heavenly light was pulling up all of the remaining demons, along with all of the lightning from the portal, into a vortex as it rose up into the dark Roman sky.

"Holy moly," I whispered to myself in awe.

The fireball and the vortex dissipated while I was still standing there, jaw agape.

"Damn, Natasha," said Michael.

As the dust cleared, literally, and the portal had faded into nearly nothing, I noticed my team were all watching in amazement like I was.

"That was quite a firecracker," remarked Alexander, probably lapsing into some of his old military lingo.

Kieran let out a wolf-whistle, similar to his whistle from much earlier that night. However, this whistle was different, slower and with a lower pitch, indicating just how impressed he was.

"Thank you, thank you," I said with a smirk.

"That was amazing to watch," marvelled Troy. "And you kept fighting. And you are still standing now!"

I looked down at the sword in my hand and smiled. I was still gaining a handle on my powers, I thought. And I was still a long way from serving their full capacities.

"I'm taking this thing home as it is," I said to myself as the group of us walked away from the now dead portal fizzling away from its spot on the Colosseum.

"We should probably report in and see what the director wants to do next," said Michael.

There was still the matter of the humans, a point made all too obvious as I heard quiet muttering and sobbing.

"They are free now," I said of them.

"I'll do a memory wipe," sighed Alexander. "While you report to Director Hask, I'll wipe their memories and we can sort out what to do next."

"Sounds like a plan," I said, taking off my armour before it became a scroll again.

"Troy, you're in charge until I get back," he said.

"I'm sorry, Alexander," Kieran said softly, looking down.

"For what?" Alexander said at first, before realizing something. "No, I was angry at Troy, for getting in my way when we first started battling. That is why I needed to stay away from him."

"What nonsense is this?" Troy snarled, taking a step towards Alexander.

"Boys, please." I stepped between them. "Not the time, nor the place. If you two need to sort out your differences later, that's fine, but for we cannot have this in the field. We need all of our strengths, and those strengths all require cooperation. Got it?"

"Thank you, Natasha," Alexander said, nodding at me.

"And?" I added, automatically, surprising myself with my newfound diplomatic skills.

"I'm sorry," Troy said first, his gaze cast vaguely in Alexander's direction.

"I'm sorry, too." Alexander's apology was directed down at his feet, but it sounded fairly genuine. "Thank you for setting us straight, Natasha."

It was at that moment, noticing the unusual deference of Alexander's nod, that I realised that I was still holding the rather large iteration of my holy sword at waist level, mindlessly running my thumb across the handle.

I quickly pointed the weapon at the ground and brought it safely to my side as I watched both men stare at me with a look in their eyes that I had never seen before.

I was not sure what that look meant, but I did notice that I was quite enjoying it.

"As Natasha said, we need to move on."

"Yeah…Alexander, you need to take care of these poor people's memories. And, in any event, I think we should get back to the director."

As we made our way up the steps of the Colosseum, I noticed the destruction that was left in the wake of our battle.

"It is a good thing we wiped their memories," said Michael, echoing my own thoughts.

There were some things even Michael would not joke about.

END OF THE LINE

Troy

Hask had enough foresight to allow us a few hours of sleep in separate rooms at the congregation's Rome headquarters. He even thought to have delivery from one of the city's better trattorias waiting for us when we reconvened in his office in the late afternoon.

As he unloaded the bags of freshly committed foodstuffs, and noted he had several local newspapers of the increasingly old-fashioned printed variety on display upon his desk.

The director's choice of printed newspapers and his more conspicuous choice of leaving them for everyone to see may have very well been his way of efficiently informing us as to what degree the press was reporting the unthinkable happenings in the midst of their city, and consequently the public's knowledge and perception of these events.

Granted, it was not the most important thing for us to spend this learning or take up our mental resources, but it was still relevant for certain. Furthermore, it took just a second or two to get a feel for the hearing on the papers amongst the greasy bags of trattoria delivery. From what I could see, the press did not really know much, certainly not of the fantastical nature of the intensity training place in Rome and other cities.

Eventi Strani seemed to be a theme amongst the headlines of the Roman papers. Simply describing the events as strange or dispari, meaning 'odd'. Maybe there was no better way to describe or contextualise such things. However, there was a distinct lack of language describing any sort of immediate danger, little less the apocalyptic nature of these events. This likely meant that the public at large had either not caught onto these things or were experiencing some mass denial of the supernatural tinge overtaking their city centers.

And I made the conscious decision to stop any concern I had with such matters as the aroma from the bags of food overtook many of the cars I had about anything.

"It's not quite the same as my cooking, but it will do," I remarked after Hask dismissed the younger congregation member, someone I did not recognise, who had led us there.

"No, there is no need to rely on scrounged together groceries tonight," Hask replied, setting up platters of gnocchi, rigatoni carbonara, and loaves of focaccia on his desk. The aroma filled the office, reminding me that I hadn't eaten since the previous day's congregation-provided lunch.

"Good," I said, deciding not to argue as I grabbed a hunk of focaccia.

"What's wrong, Troy?" Hask asked as I took a huge bite. "You look perturbed."

Was he reading my mind, or did he just know me so well? I wondered as I swallowed my mouthful of bread.

He could have been referring to the apocalyptic bout we had just been a part of back in the Colosseum, but that would have been too obvious.

"I am just fine," I said, picking up a bottle of Peroni from the foam cooler on the floor and pretending to study the label. "Or at least, I will be."

Hask and I looked at each expectantly, waiting for the other to elaborate.

He was quicker on the draw.

"I hear your cooking is quite marvellous indeed, Troy."

Both Alexander and myself instantly looked over at Natasha who was looking straight down at the plate of gnocchi on her lap as if she were ashamed of something. She had clearly complimented my cooking while speaking to Hask about our team's life at the flat. Why Alexander looked at Natasha, then actually looked over at me, as if he were mildly upset about something, I could never guess.

"Uh, let us discuss your next mission," Hask announced, looking displeased with the weird little moment he had inadvertently created.

It was an odd enough scene already, with all of us eating decent local food from paper plates in Hask's office.

There were surely reasons Director Hask had for wanting to avoid the commissary.

"What's next, boss?" Michael asked with his mouth full of what must have been the finest carbonara he had ever had.

"You will be heading to the portal in Madrid. We believe it may be around one of the metro stations on one of the lines there."

"That narrows it down." Michael punctuated his comment with a swig of beer. For once, I agreed with the sentiment of his jesting.

"Why Madrid?" I asked.

"Been some curious activity in the area," Hask answered. "More than normal, even for hell's heartbeat."

This got Alexander's attention.

"What's that mean?" he asked point blank.

Hask gave him a look we all recognised, it was a look that said Alexander was chasing an unproductive line of questioning.

"It means, whoever is using the portal has been coming and going with more frequency than usual."

"More than that Book of Revelations recreation we saw being played out last night?" I asked.

"You will soon be on your way there to find out. Now off you go, you have got a long journey from Roma Tiburtina ahead of you."

We thanked Hask and vacated his office, I looked back as the door shut.

He was already swivelling in his chair to stare at the giant monitor on his wall that displayed colourful maps of the world with various locations highlighted in red and green.

Our driver was not Mrs. Beatrice that time, but someone who I had guessed Hask had hired just for transportation purposes. The youngish, perpetually silent man, not only did he take us to the station but he accompanied us all the way to the platform with heavy footed steps. The last stirrings of dusk were still present outside, and what seemed to be our train was starting to pull slowly up to the platform.

Alexander gave our heavy bags a shove with his foot to position them closer to where it seemed like the door to the sleeper car would end up on the platform.

It was only when the train came to a full stop that I realised there were about twenty people or so waiting for us on board.

It was a quiet, somber boarding, for both my team and the scattered other travellers.

From what I had gathered there was still an air of mystery surrounding the happenings at the colosseum that morning, but there must have been an overall sense of dread in the air inspired by the news coming in from all over Europe.

By the time we had started moving, it served as though Natasha, Kieran, and Michael had all retreated to their private cabins.

A few of the other passengers immediately took refuge in

the next car over—which was the dining car, at least appeared to be from the few brief glimpses I saw from the doorway opening and closing.

What no one seemed to elect to do was sit in the small, open array of seats in what appeared to be a lounge section of sorts, just past the sleeping compartments.

So, naturally, I chose to spend some time there.

I sat alone quietly in my seat by the window, watching as we passed through the night time cityscape outside.

"She must really enjoy your cooking."

Sure, I was able to stop myself from jumping at the sound of Alexander's voice, but it had startled me enough that I came close.

"What? Are you still thinking about Hask's innocuous little comment?" I asked Alexander defensively before glancing in his direction just long enough to see him almost glaring at me from a seat across the aisle.

I turned my attention away from the view outside of the train window, a view with which I had been thoroughly engrossed, to face Alexander, understanding that he wished to have a conversation.

"It seems as though you're the only one she chooses to talk to about to others." Alexander looked to be close to seething by that point. If I hadn't known better, I would have guessed that his feelings were so hurt that he was just sharing them unfiltered.

"Alexander, I know that you cannot be this petty about things."

"Petty? You really have a way with words, don't you? Honestly, I am not being petty. I am just stating facts and drawing conclusions from them. Facts and conclusions that apparently you are too thick skulled to make yourself."

He looked hurt. He looked, and again this was something I would have liked to think beneath him, but he looked jealous.

Yet if he were jealous indeed, I knew accusing him of such was not going to help matters in any immediate way, so the best I could do is try to find some common ground.

"She really is something special, is she not?" I began.

Alexander simply had to agree with that, I figured.

"Yes, she is. I care about her a great deal. And, what I cannot hide, even from you, especially from you, Troy, is that I care not only about her but for her. I care for her very much."

That caught me off guard, and yet it didn't. I knew he cared for her in some way that was different than me, but I did not expect him to admit to it like this. Not to me, at least.

And not in such a fragile way.

"I know you do." I tried to reassure him. "You always have."

"But now someone else does, that she returns those feelings to… it…"

"No, not someone else. Just you. You're special to her, even if it isn't in that way."

I saw a hint of a smile appear on his face as I said that.

"Thank you, Troy," he said, "I appreciate that."

I smiled back at him.

"You're welcome, my friend. After all, we both realise what is most important, it is not your feelings, and it certainly is not mine."

"Yes," he said quietly. "It is Natasha who truly matters. And I would never want to do anything that would jeopardise her safety or her happiness."

I nodded and the conversation died down again. Being in the presence of Alexander or any of my teammates always had a way of making me slightly more aware of my own situation, my thoughts and motivations, even if the less pleasant and painful facets of these things were the facets I had successfully managed to forget for a while.

"Thank you," I said to Alexander.

"For what?" he scoffed slightly, but before there tension between us could start rebuilding itself he found his way quickly back to our common ground.

"Natasha is getting some rest, the last I noticed."

"Yes, I saw her sleeping."

"She looked very tired, it's been a rough few days. And I cannot fathom that a blast like that could not have seriously taken it out of her, despite her outward demeanour about it. Like all of us, she will need to be fully alert for Madrid, especially as this is another case in such the exact portal location of a mystery."

"We will all need to be at full capacity, indeed. Do you know how large Madrid's transit system is? If the portal is even by the metro as Hask surmised."

Alexander smiled at me briefly then turned his eyes back to staring out the window. He didn't seem to have anything else to say so I let the silence linger for a while.

"You know," I said, trying to break the silence.

"What?" he asked, turning back to me again.

"We're going to be together a lot more from now on."

Finally, I thought, maybe he'd realised that his cold shoulder routine wasn't going to help him with me or the team, and he'd start being normal. That would have made things so much easier.

"I know," he said in a flat confirmation that what I said was true. However, he was just starting to signal that he was losing interest, even with this subject which seemed to enthral us both so.

Kieran and Michael were still nowhere to be found, and Natasha was still dead asleep. Even if I could not see her at that very moment, I could somehow just sense her resting in blissful peace in her compartment nearby.

Yet I was wide awake, and so was Alexander, so for a touch more conversation I was going to have to find a different tactic.

"She inspires me," I said at last. "She may be the bravest one out of all of us."

"I know," Alexander repeated. The words were the same as his last reply, but his tone had changed to something softer, something more open, and something much more genuine. "She inspires me, too."

While the air of the train ride did not have that odd magic of our earlier overnight ride from Paris to Zurich, the Madrid-bound train did take in a peaceful air after Alexander and I aired out tensions—or rather he had aired his tension.

"Hey, where's Natasha?" I asked, looking around for my slumbering colleague.

"She said she was going back to her room,"Alexander replied. "She looked pretty beat."

"Yeah, she was," I agreed. "I don't know how she does it time and again."

I got up from my seat and walked over to the hallway that led to the sleeper compartments where Natasha was supposed to be resting.

The train droned on, and I soon found myself standing outside the door to the private room that Natasha had been given. Unlike my own room in the passenger car, hers had a tiny window that looked out onto the darkened rural scene somewhere between northern Italy and southern France. I knocked on the door and waited. No answer. I knocked again, longer this time.

"Why do you wish to wake her?" This latest odyssey with my team had certainly brought with it things with which I was not accustomed. Hearing Alexander use a gentle tone was the most astonishing of those things.

I turned to see him leaning against the frame of the open door to his own room, one hand in his pocket and a faint smile on his lips.

"Hask told us to rest," I said, knowing that he was fully

aware of why I had come. "She's probably really tired, must be more than any one of us."

Alexander laughed softly and pushed himself off of his doorway.

"It sounds as if you are explaining why you shouldn't be waking her." Of course, Alexander was correct. There was no halfway reasonable excuse I could muster, so I had grabbed at the first reasonable excuse that surfaced in my mind. And Alexander and I were both fully aware of that.

I wanted to turn around and go back to my room, but something about Alexander's insistence made me stay put. I didn't want to risk making him mad for some reason.

"Go ahead," he urged me. "She won't bite, unless that's what you want."

As I lifted my left boot off the ground and readied myself to take a step towards where Alexander stood in the door frame of his sleeper compartment, I could not help but note that the look of mild amusement on his mug had seemed to grow into an even wider self-satisfied simper. Whilst my first instinct was to allow this to infuriate me further, when I had realised the reason for Alexander's amusement I felt the traces of a smile on my own lips. Even while stepping heavily towards him, I was still moving gently so as to not waken Natasha.

"Very droll, Alexander," I whispered down to him as I passed him by.

The car was dark, save for the moonlight coming in through the windows, and quietly lit by the lights of the passing stations. Even with the relative brightness of the passing stations, it still took a few moments for my eyes to adjust to the darkness.

The physical dimension to my tiredness hit me like a ten tonne weight as I passed through the open seating section of the train car once more. It was enough that there was no resisting the urge to sit down and give my eyes and body what I figured to be a few minutes, at most, of rest. Even with my own reserved sleeping compartment just a few meters away, it was one of those sudden onslaughts of suppressed fatigue making itself known.

I just had to sit down.

A moment later, my head was laying against the cold glass of the window, and my eyes were closing.

I woke up to the dull blare of the train intercom, and the feeling of Natasha shaking my shoulder to wake me. I turned to her as she dug around in her purse for something.

"What time is it?" I groaned in a voice I barely recognised as my own, my tongue feeling like sandpaper.

She turned to me, a small bottle of painkillers in hand.

"It's about half past four, you need these," she said, handing me the bottle.

I sat up and twisted the cap off the medicine, then took two of the pills before washing them down with the bottled water she handed me next.

"Thanks."

As my eyes and mind focused enough to take in a look of that open section of the train car, I noted that Natasha and I were the only members of my team currently awake. And I knew that because Kieran, Michael, and Alexander were all visibly slumbering in seats across from us. It also appeared that Natasha was the only one who had spent the bulk of the ride in her compartment.

Everyone else, as far as I could tell, had been in the common section at some point. There was not much mystery to it. Natasha was the only member of the team exhausted enough to stave off the anxious insomnia that had driven the rest of us to wander through the train at some point.

Sitting up, I looked to Natasha. She wore a green and blue plaid shirt with blue jeans and hiking boots, with a slim leather belt around her waist. It was a far cry from the garb she had donned in Rome.

"I don't even think I heard you guys fighting," Natasha whispered, tilting her head in the direction of Alexander slumbering across the aisle.

"Were you expecting to hear that?" I rubbed my own temples lightly.

Natasha's warm, glowing smile told me that I was taking her all too seriously, or at the very least too literally.

"I'm glad you're able to exist in the same room again," she whispered, her continued smile telling me that was exaggerating for humorous effect.

Letting out a barely audible chuckle, I noticed there was still no hint of early morning light through the windows on either side of the train, despite the reality of us hurtling through central Spain on our way to Madrid in the middle of summer.

"It's still dark out," I mentioned to her, feeling a bit like the broken record I had become on the ever-lightless train.

Her eyes flicked upwards as if she were staring through the train car's ceiling to the world outside.

"There's no sunlight coming from up there, either." Natasha and I both looked in the direction of the recently awakened Michael, who was in the midst of his first wisecrack of the day. "Even if you could see through the ceiling."

The lighthearted barb was met with total silence from both of us, and even the snoring racket that had previously been reverberating from across the room had ceased.

"I should express some gratitude for that." That time it was Alexander, who just like Michael had awakened and decided to immediately join in on the conversation.

"No rest for the wicked and all that," Alexander continued, looking in my direction with a joke that did not quite make sense but was clearly an attempt to show some reconciliation between us. Natasha traveled to Alexander and then back to me, the corners of her lips turned just enough to show that was pleased with that development.

"You're telling me." And then there was Kieran, the last of our team to awaken, sharing a mild complaint.

"You could have stayed in your compartment," Michael responded with a laugh.

"We all could have," Kieran stated, quite correctly, with a yawn. "Also, I suppose we can speak with normal voices now."

Kieran was naturally still whispering as he noted this.

He was right, as the snoring that had once permeated the whole room had ceased. Strangely enough, our normal speaking voices may have been quieter.

Also stranger was that the moment all of us were awake was followed shortly by the moment in which what little conversation there was between us seemed to cease. Instead of studying the faces of my teammates to deduce what they may have been thinking, I instead focused on my thoughts. As the train blew through some station without stopping, my mind went to thoughts of those responsible for all of these portals, those who had seemed conspicuously absent from our last couple adventures.

"Haven't heard from our old friends for a while." Michael broke the silence as the train sped away from the well-lit station and back into the relative darkness.

With that comment, Michael confirmed that his thoughts were the same as mine. Of course, he was referring to no friend of ours, but rather the closest thing our team had to a rival.

"Zavier," Natasha said with a strange laugh that sounded to be bursting with disgust. "Him and his demon daddy. What's his name? Kevin?"

"You know it's Kalgin," I laughed.

"And that's what I'm talking about."

"We haven't seen them in a while," she said somewhat defensively. "Maybe they moved on with their lives or something."

"Well if they did, they were the only ones," I said, looking out the window to the darkness rushing past.

This dry humour seemed to have been affecting the whole team. Truth be told there were two reported portals left, including the one we were headed to in Madrid, and if Zavier and his high demon priest patriarch, Kalgin, were not somehow skulking around there, we would need to deal with them soon enough.

"If we find them in this last portal..." Michael started to say.

"Then we send them back to where they came from," Natasha finished.

"After all," Natasha added, "now we know for sure that it's them. I know some of the fairies had been jerk faces to Troy, but that doesn't mean..."

"Nothing is certain. It's become clear at least some fae are involved. After that fight, in Switzerland, some of them just told us outright." The words came out flatly, words I wanted not to have to say at all, but felt it necessary to say to finish the seemingly incomplete picture Natasha had of the situation.

Natasha trailed off as she sensed the discomfort from the rest of us. She had been unconscious during my exchange with the fae from my old kingdom.

In fact, I felt as though I needed to explain that little wrinkle to everyone.

"Troy, why didn't you say anything about this before..."

Those few moments in the cemetery in Zurich were not moments I wanted to replay in my memory: holding Natasha after she'd nearly fallen to the ground, my heart full of worry for her. It was the worst state to be in as fae folks from my former kingdom revealed that not only were they working for the side of Kalgin and his minions but were possibly doing so at the behest of my father.

It confounded me as to how not only the denizens, but

the leadership could have been collaborating somehow with the darkest of evil forces known anywhere.

As far removed as I thought I had been from the concerns of the kingdom for so long, that idea continued to upset me for reasons I could not articulate and, on that train with my teammates, had no intentions of exploring.

All I could do was try to get out of that facet of conversation as efficiently as I could.

"I thought it would just be best not to discuss it."

"Why would you think that?"

"Look, we don't have time for this," I said as I glared out the window. "I told you that some of the fae were working with demons. We can talk about this later."

To me, that seemed to wrap up that conversation.

"I've been meaning to ask you something about that." Natasha, in her insistence on continuing, showed my assumption that the conversation was over to be dead wrong.

"Go ahead," I offered, trying not to sound too reticent.

"Isn't there some, well, power vacuum now. In your old kingdom, I mean? I was just wondering about your father, if you knew anything that was happening with that."

That sounded a lot worse than just a simple question about the fae kingdom.Thinking about my father inevitably meant thinking about so many things from the past, and in this case the present, that I'd rather avoid, so I avoided the issue altogether whenever possible.

But if she was asking, then she must have been aware of the situation in some way.

"If you remember that... fellow, I guess you could call him, back in Zurich."

Natasha's face only showed confusion. After all, that had been such a small part of the many ordeals we had faced.

"Your friend Henry!" Michael shouted gleefully.

"Oh, right," Natasha said softly.

"Not my friend," I corrected Michael. "And not 'Henry' for certain. But, there were more of him, more of them, I would say. The fae we saw in Zurich."

"Oh, so you didn't quite dispatch them all?"

I looked at the ground, then back in her eyes. To me this felt like a challenge, though her face showed only curiosity. I don't think she knew what she was getting into with that stare.

"We were a little preoccupied," I exhaled. "Look, I don't want to talk about it."

I looked around the compartment. Everyone was staring at me.

"My father is still on his throne, if not literally," I continued. "And he might be a bit closer to Zavier's father than I realised."

"What are you saying?" Natasha asked.

"It was quite explicit." There was a sensation which felt almost like a tear as I continued to explain as clearly as I could. "The fae there made it clear whose side they're on, which side my father, their king is on. And it's not our side."

"So what, are you afraid of fairies now?" she scowled.

I was a little taken back.

"We should tell Hask," she continued. "He'll know what to do."

I saw a flicker of doubt cross her face, but she didn't say anything else. I think the truth was we were all a little afraid, not just of the existential threat the dark magic ritual posed to the world we all knew, but of our apparent and growing roles as central figures in this epoch-making struggle.

As for myself, the protective wall that I had built around my mind and my heart, a wall which had been built up over centuries and continuously hardened and reinforced, looked like it was going to need to come down no matter how sturdy and deep I had tried to lay its foundations. It was the wall protecting me from dealing with those things I'd chosen to leave buried in the depths of the past.

"That is what they told Troy," Alexander confirmed. "Although I had thought it to be so much nonsense. Why haven't you shared this with Hask?"

"Honestly, I hadn't thought to. I haven't been thinking about this at all. I don't...I can't."

I felt Natasha's hand touching my knee lightly.

She seemed to realise how sore this all was for me. She seemed to understand it much better than even I understood it.

Alexander seemed to briefly look away. I couldn't tell if it was because he didn't want to intrude or if there was another reason.

"Well, we're almost there anyway," she said.

I wasn't sure who she was trying to convince.

"There is no point in telling Hask for his advice alone," I stated flatly. "There is only one thing for this. I'm going to need to talk to my dad." Nobody argued.

"It's only been five-hundred years or so." And nobody laughed, because that was true.

The train stopped at a platform that looked as if it was from the Victorian era. It was almost as if the technological clock had been set back here.

The four of us stood from our seats, collected our things, and proceeded off the train. I looked behind me as the train left the station and saw nobody waiting for us.

Stepping from the train car and getting a better look at the space, it became clear that much of the architecture had been updated to a more modern styling, with a steel and glass ceiling high above the cavernous terminal and escalators leading up from the track on which we'd arrived.

However, the escalators were not running. The station looked empty and barren, with only the occasional soft echoes of stray footsteps coming from far off corners of the building.

"Madrid," the conductor called from the open door of the train car behind us, his accent infused with traces of both Spain and Italy. His announcement was curious as everyone had disembarked by then and it was clearly the end of the line.

Looking at Natasha, Alexander, and the rest of my team surrounded by our luggage next to the train which had taken us from Rome, I felt a tremendous guilt at leaving them at that moment. But, this was something I couldn't put off as Kalgin and his minions threatened the apocalypse.

"Take care of her," were my last words before finding a private spot to create a portal to the Kingdom of the Fae.

13

A SLIVER OF DARKNESS

Natasha

After his justification, which seemed at one both forced and perfectly believable, Troy just left us there in the Madrid train station to go create a magic circle to the Kingdom of the Fae. As important as he seemed to think that was, he left Alexander, Kieran, Michael, and I standing in the train terminal literally holding our bags.

"What did he say?" is all I could ask after Troy walked off into some dark corner of the station.

"He said we need to stick together," Alexander responded, staring off into some distance. "Or something like that."

"I can't get a signal here," Kieran exclaimed, poking at his phone. "Hask messaged me to hire a hotel suite and expense report it, which I did, but…"

"We need to find the portal," Alexander growled, letting whatever frustration he was feeling build.

"We need to find the suite I just booked," replied Kieran.

"Kieran's right." I picked up my bags. "We need to get you back to the hotel, wherever it is, before daybreak." I pointed to Alexander.

"You might want to hurry."

The three of us walked over to the exit of the train station. I spared a glance over my shoulder and saw Alexander still in the middle of the space, growling.

"I don't understand," I said. "Is he coming?"

Kieran whipped his head around.

"You're the one we're hurrying for," he shouted over to Alexander.

Alexander lingered inside, nearly still and looking as if he were studying one of the massive, leafy plants on display in the middle of the station's main floor. What he was actually ruminating on was anybody's guess.

"I don't have time for this," I said.

"It's not that he'll disappear off the face of the Earth if he stays out after dark, but you know how it is. Sunlight hurts. It actually burns."

"So does acid. Let's not even get started on what freaking airplanes do to you," Kieran said, imitating being burned.

We were both actually addressing Alexander, knowing he could hear us clearly, as a way to get some reaction and movement from the traditionally the most active and imperious member of the team.

"Okay, the pair of you have officially lost it," I said.

"Look, let's just get this over with."

"Are you sure, Natasha?"

"I'm sure. We're wasting time."

Grumbling under his breath, Kieran followed me out of the alley and onto the open street.

It was a pleasant, cool predawn, with the moon looking nearly full apart from a lingering dark sliver. Still, Alexander would be feeling the burn any minute now.

"You coming, big guy?" I heard Michael yelling a few meters behind us, followed by Alexander's distinctive footfalls. Apparently, that was what it took to get Alexander to snap the hell out of it.

"Right this way." Kieran gestured for us to follow him down the narrow street just outside Madrid-Chamartin Station. He was taking his phone back out of his pocket.

"I thought you lost the address when your phone went dead," I said while following him along with Alexander and Michael.

"I could tell it was close by," Kieran answered with unusual confidence past a taxi stand towards a five-story brutalist glass and concrete building just adjacent to the station.

"Yes, this is the hotel, alright," Kieran confirmed out loud upon checking his phone. For once, he was in control and the rest of us continued to follow him silently.

We walked along the cracked pavement path leading into the hotel. The air became refreshingly chilly after we followed Kieran through the revolving door into the lobby. While the walk to the hotel had been quiet enough, with no noises but the hum of traffic in the background, the hotel lobby was even more peaceful. Not quite ominously quiet, but bordering on unsettling as we approached the front desk.

"Buenos días, gente encantadora," the woman at the front desk greeted us warmly and a bit familiarly.

She had a dark brown complexion and long curly hair with lightly tanned features. Her shimmering maroon-coloured dress fit in well with the elegant dark wooden furniture and ivory walls of the hotel lobby.

"Hablas inglés?" Kieran asked with a somewhat endearing over-formality.

"Of course, sir," she responded with a mixture of surprise and amusement.

"We have a reservation under the name, uh, hang on." As Kieran started tapping at his phone to find whatever name he'd used to reserve our suite, the woman's face seemed to be fighting the urge to show any trace of confusion. After

Michael tried to cover up a guffaw by clearing his throat, the hotel desk lady's features fell back into a warm smile.

"Ah, yes," declared Kieran. "The name is Smithers...Peter Smithers."

"Yes, Mr. Smithers," she started. "Your rooms are ready for you. Will you be needing rooms for the rest of the week?"

"Ah, yes, madame. For the rest of the week...for now," he responded. "How much per night?"

Michael had to pretend-cough hard to cover up another laugh.

"Four hundred euros a night, Mr. Smithers," she stated clearly without betraying any emotion. "We've already charged the deposit to the card on file."

Kieran looked at the rest of us with a 'shall we continue?' face, and we all nodded.

"Of course, Mr. Smithers," the lady stated. "Feel free to take the lift to your left up to your rooms."

"Ah, yes, thank you," he said as we all walked towards the lifts.

The woman gave us a quick nod and smile as the glass doors shut in front of us.

"So...Peter Smithers?" I asked once we were alone in the elevator.

"Dude, I know right!" Michael shouted from behind me. "I couldn't believe it!"

"It was perfect," Kieran replied proudly, perhaps mistaking Michael's amusement for flattery.

"Wouldn't the real Peter Smithers be able to recognize his own name?" asked Alexander. I have to admit I felt more than a modicum of relief that he had decided to break the silent treatment he had been giving us since our arrival in Madrid.

Kieran did not bother to answer straight away, but there was a resonant dinging sound as the lift doors opened on the fourth floor, where I could only assume our suite was located.

"Well, come on," he said, not really answering the question but clearly expecting us to follow him out of the lift.

It was only then that I realized how exhausted I still felt. I had been running on adrenaline for the last forty-eight hours and I had slept for maybe six of those. What I had not shared with my teammates was that I had laid awake for most of the night after our battle in Rome, not to mention on our train ride to Madrid. All the extra energy I may have banked sleeping for those past few days seemed to have been depleted almost completely. I slumped against the side of the lift in an effort to prop myself up and reach some sort of standing position.

I couldn't let my team see me like this. They would ask questions that I couldn't answer, and I hated not seeming prepared and in control.

I stumbled forward, blinded by the harsh light, as the doors opened to reveal a well-lit and luxurious hallway. There were two doors either side of the hall with a mirror and coat stand in the middle. Two stone statues stood on either side of a dark wooden door at the very end of the hallway.

I squinted, trying to make out more details of the statues in the bright light. It looked as though they were holding some sort of weapon in their hands but from where I was standing I couldn't quite tell.

The boys didn't seem to notice the statues as they were now admiring the surprisingly spacious and well-appointed suite as they wandered into it. I followed behind them, dragging my feet as I tried not to drop onto the floor.

Dawn was surely breaking outside in Madrid, and it would be hours before it would be safe for Alexander to venture back outside with us regardless.

"The hunter needs to rest," I said, slurring my words, fully aware I was making no bloody sense as I half-dragged myself down the hallway. "But the hunted always seeks its prey. So it seeks itself, or something. Whatever, I'm going to sleep before you lot get yourselves into trouble without me."

Michael, Kieran, and Alexander made no effort to reply even if they had heard me; they were too busy closing the curtains and dragging their luggage into the various rooms of the suite.

I managed to slowly peel off my lavender silk summer scarf, dropping it onto the floor of one of the empty bedrooms as I stumbled into the ensuite and collapsed into bed.

I tried to remain awake, fully intending on waiting for the others to fall asleep so I could wander the suite and maybe research some more about the whereabouts of this magic portal, but I was just so exhausted from our trip that I fell fast asleep no more than a minute after my head hit the pillow.

When I opened my eyes, feeling terrifically refreshed, I was mildly disappointed to see a shaft of sunlight still shining through the curtains of the room. I could not have slept for too long. When I saw the digital display on the clock radio next to the bed, I was almost inspired to start.

It was only eleven bloody thirty still.

After silently reassuring myself that I felt rested enough, I stumbled into the en-suite, showered, and dressed in one of the last fresh sets of clothes I had packed.

I re-entered the bedroom to find that the lads were still asleep so I took the opportunity to have a look through the other rooms in the hopes of finding something relating to our mission.

The main room had an expensive looking laptop on a coffee table, with a leather lounge and a large flat screen TV, although there wasn't anything on it. It was safe to assume that Kieran had brought it there.

"It is still morning, isn't it?" Alexander's voice was not much of a surprise to hear—the curtains in the hotel suite were all still tightly drawn as not to let in the sun, and the team all seemed to be suffering from acute insomnia.

"Definitely," answered Kieran, whose voice I also heard before turning around to see those two along with Michael, all awake as I was, lingering about the suite.

"Just give it some time, we'll have the whole day to check out the city. You need the sleep, Natasha. You have been releasing more firepower in the past week than you ever have in your life. Your body still needs rest."

"I'm already feeling a little more with it now," I said in partial lie. "But I think I'll pass on breakfast; I might just go for a walk around the block or something."

I figured that I would not call out Alexander on his faulty logic—he could not work with us all day since he was a vampire—and he would return the favor by not trying to call me out for having no real reason to venture around Madrid on my own.

Despite being intelligent and observant, all of the team did have a tendency to think that I was just some frail girl who needed looking after. If I was going to be looked after, I would rather it be for a more substantial reason than just my non-boy status. After brushing my teeth and combing through my long-suffering hair, I strode swiftly towards the door of our hotel suite with no set plan.

"Where are you going so fast, Natasha?"

Kieran put a crimp in my half-baked notion by questioning it.

He was sitting on a leather sectional near the suite door, along with Michael and Alexander. They were all nursing mugs of coffee from the suite's French press, and as I saw them I realized they were staring straight at me as I was trying to essentially run out the door. Kieran's entertained little half-smile told me that he knew I could not think of an excuse if I wanted.

"You're not going to go searching Madrid for the portal on your own, are you?" The simper remained on his face as he asked.

If Kieran was amused, I expected Michael to be on the verge of breaking into hysterics. Yet, as my eyes traveled over to his I saw a surprising concern.

"I know we're already missing one team member," he said, referring to Troy who had gone to the fae kingdom to confront his father. "We don't want to lose another."

The unexpected wash of kindness from Michael had tears almost about to form, and I blinked hard to hold them back.

"Hey, hey," Michael continued. "It's okay. Troy's right here."

And indeed, Michael had shifted into the shape of Troy to cheer me up.

He gave me a humorously overwrought and earnest pep talk in the style of Troy:

"There is a term the fairy-folk in my old kingdom use, Natasha, to describe the type of men our teammates are. That ancient term is 'schmucks'. While these schmucks, as they would be known in my realm, may not possess your angelic beauty nor my exquisite taste in ball caps, it is advisable to let a couple of them go with you as you traipse about Madrid." As much as I wanted to laugh, there was a strange sadness holding back my smile. At least, until Michael continued: "And above all, remember you are good at what you do. You can handle anything."

There was no fighting the smile I felt spreading across my face after that.

Any nascent tears had fully dried by the time Kieran and Michael had deposited their mugs on the coffee table and risen to come join my search for the portal in Madrid.

I noticed Alexander was standing as well.

"You…you cannot be considering joining us as well."

"You know I can't." Alexander grinned warmly as he stepped closer to me. "But I just wanted to remind you that our team could never do without you. So please, be careful."

After a final step towards me Alexander leaned down to punctuate his words with a soft kiss upon my forehead.

I bit back a giggle as the red in his cheeks grew darker, but he took a gentlemanly step back to regard me, his eyes full of friendly affection, admiration, and, yes, respect.

"Alright, alright." Michael called. "The mushy stuff can wait until after the mission. We're one Troy down as it is and Alexander can't even come with us. Kieran, we'll need you to start leading the way."

Kieran's eyes widened adorably as Michael pointed towards him.

"Me?"

"Yes you," Michael confirmed. "You're good at this stuff. We need that lycanthrope nose of yours, buddy."

Kieran looked at me as if he needed final approval, which I did grant him with a slight smile and a hearty nod.

"Then let's go." Kieran puffed his chest, reminding me a bit of how well-toned and muscular it's always been, and swaggered towards the door of the suite.

"Kieran," I called.

"Yeah?"

"Do you think they're here? I mean, if, when we find the portal, will we need to deal with… you know."

His eyes opened a bit as he considered his answer. "Um… it's possible. But according to Hask's intel, there's at least one more portal besides the one here in Madrid. But, if they're about, well, we should be able to handle them. Because…"

"Because we'll have no other choice," Michael said, finishing Kieran's sentence.

"We're not here to fight the big cheese and his half-demon little cheese," Michael continued. "But if we have to, we will."

I had to look over to Alexander, who was subtly grinding his jaw and shifting his weight from one foot to the other, naturally unable to bear the idea of letting us face that fight alone, if it came to it.

"If it comes to it, I will find a way to do whatever needs to be done." Alexander sat back down, his eyes looking focused and confident at the thought of possibly having to risk his own safety if necessary. "Kieran, make sure your phone is charged so you can keep me apprised."

"Oh, it is charged," Kieran held up the device. "And my nose is charged, too," he jested.

"Whatever happens, we need the portals shut before they get the chance to invade."

I looked at the two and could see on their faces that this was much more than just an assignment to them. It was to all of us. This meant everything to every soul in existence who had anything to exist for.

There was a renewed sense of purpose I could feel in the air amongst all of us as Michael and I followed Kieran out of the suite and towards the hotel lift.

"Any hunches yet?" I asked Kieran.

"Only what Hask mentioned about the Madrid transit system," Kieran answered without turning around, focused on summoning the lift and leading the way.

"I think that's the most likely place to check, but I wouldn't discount any of the other places."

"What do you mean?" I asked. "Did Hask mention other places in Madrid?"

"I meant the other portals. So far, they're all very public places," Kieran explained as the lift doors opened and were boarded. "And the big cheese, as Michael calls him, is going to want to send large waves of demons through at a time, as fast as possible, to collect maximal souls as Hask told us."

"So you think it is more likely to be there?" I asked. "Or

are you all still following the lead of what Emilio told us. Because, you know, the power of suggestion and all that."

"You know what the tube is like in London, right?" Kieran asked as he, Michael, and I formed a huddle as the lift took us down to the lobby.

"Of course." I smirked. "It can't be nearly that crowded on the Madrid metro. Can it?"

Michael and Kieran shared a look. "Imagine that crowded, or more," Michael began, "and smaller stations, and no English over-politeness."

I considered this as the elevator slowly lowered to the lobby floor. "Surely people still say excuse me if they accidentally bump into one another."

"Maybe," said Michael. "But there's less of a general awareness of personal space. It's part of the Spanish culture to be closer to one another. To share one another's air, as it were. Like this." He took a step toward me, and before I could back away he leaned in close to my face.

Kieran and Michael both started laughing loudly as the lift doors opened.

"Let's just say things are prone towards chaos already," Michael said as we stepped out into the still empty hotel lobby.

"They've done their research," I added, considering the various portal locations and what they signified.

"There may have been ritualistic reasons for the other portals," Kieran started explaining in a hushed voice as we walked past the bored front desk lady. "But they've all been tactical, too. We really don't know yet, or at least I don't."

Despite his words, Kieran's body language betrayed some intuition as he marched straight through the revolving door and made an immediate left turn onto the pavement. Michael and I followed him without question, walking slightly behind as Kieran led us through the midday Madrid sun, leaning subtly forward with his nose angled ahead of him.

It was not clear whether Kieran was taking his reputation for sniffing things out a bit literally, or he was just relying on his superior olfactory out of habit, or as part of some mélange of canine instinct buried deep within him.

It was probably all of the above.

Michael and I shared a glance as we walked next to each other behind Kieran. While neither of us spoke, letting our teammate concentrate, we seemed to share the same uncertainty about this blind search around Madrid on foot.

I ran my hand lightly over my satchel containing my magic feather and scroll, hoping I would not be needing those items anytime soon. I also had what was left of the magical healing blanket, but the possible need for that seemed remote at best.

Still, I found myself whispering, "God forbid," as we followed Kieran's lead, almost backtracking on ourselves to reach a quieter, almost deserted side street.

Kieran had slowed his pace and was already sniffing at the air. He stopped and tilted his head as he tried to make sense of which way the scent was blowing.

"Got something?" Michael asked.

"I do," Kieran replied quickly, a little too with purpose. "It's faint, but I know it."

"You sure?"

"Yes," he said. "Come on."

Kieran turned down a narrow alley between two buildings. We followed closely. The alley was long. At the end of it was a large metal door, with a sign on it reading: *No entry*.

"It's in English," I said quietly. Kieran turned towards us and nodded as if to say: *I noticed, and that did seem strange.*

"So what?" Michael scoffed loudly. "That doesn't mean a thing."

"Maybe it's not important." I was still whispering,

partially to indicate to Michael that it was better to be safe than sorry.

Kieran slowly approached the door. It was heavy and metal, with a wheel at the bottom for lifting it. He sniffed around the doorframe before walking in a slow circle around the outside of the door.

"It's here," he said, more to himself than anyone else. "This is where they're coming through."

"What is this building?" I asked, my voice growing quieter although I was not even sure what the purpose of that was. "Is it anything to do with the metro here, or?"

My words, my actions, were starting to make less sense to me as I observed them. It felt like the side-effects of my sleep deficit, maybe. Or something else.

"I'm going inside," he said, disappearing through the door with a quickness that seemed to defy the laws of physics.

"No, wait!" I called out, following him through.

The darkness vanished as light flooded into my eyes. As my vision returned to me, I saw we were in a large room with a high ceiling and a long counter. Behind the counter was a security guard, snoozing in his chair. We were not alone.

A man in a dark, hooded robe stood staring at us. His eyes were not like my eyes, nor my teammates' eyes nor anything with a vestige of humanity; there was no white, only blackness. Two black holes, drawing my gaze in as I could not look anywhere else.

Even as the horribly familiar sounds of panic and chaos were starting to erupt from somewhere beneath the floor where I stood, and somewhere in the distance in front of me, I could not look away.

Eyes like two portals into an abyss I had fallen down once before. Eyes that had looked upon the very same scenes of chaos and destruction I had witnessed, in battle, in nightmares, in the dreadful daydreams which arose during the worst moments of anxiety, and relished in all of them. Eyes that had been closed for decades, but were now open again. I stepped back instinctively, bumping into someone, or rather something, as I did so.

It was not a pleasant experience.

I took another step back, and bumped into something else, and then something else again.

It felt as though the very walls of the room were breathing and shifting form as the sounds of mass panic ebbed and flowed from all directions.

Yet my eyes were still drawn to those two black holes. I could not catch sight of my teammates; I could not tell what was real. The sounds faded and I felt the space around me open up again as everything faded like a bad dream.

Everything, that was, except for the figure and its two black holes that my eyes were unable to escape.

"So..."

That voice.

I had never in all my years encountered such a voice. It surely belonged to a demon, that was certain, but it was higher than any I had heard before, effeminate even, yet with a grumbling, almost subsonic undertone which shook the world around it. It was cold and dark like the abyss, and just as unforgiving. I could not see its face, yet I knew those eyes would be staring at me, sizing me up as they had done before. His presence seemed to command the very air around him to tremble in fear as it continued.

"...you're the angel that's been causing me so much trouble."

14

THE DEMON'S RATIONALE

Zavier

You would think that a demon as intelligent and cunning as my father would not fall for the same tricks twice, let alone three or four times. He may have argued, if confronted on the matter, that everything was falling into place perfectly, somehow.

The reality of Paris, and of Zurich, ran counter to that, and then Madrid, too, fell to pieces.

The angel and her allies had ensured that the plan succeeded. My father may have been able to salvage something, with the aid of my previous successes, if he had stopped there. Yet he did not, and so it all fell apart.

It was easy enough to see, from some wrongheaded prerogative, of course, that he was a slave, a slave to his own pride on one hand and the whims of the angel on the other. He could have let victory ensue in Zurich, at least that's what it appeared to me when I made the mistake of trying to understand the larger machinations at play.

Yet, I realised, that was my own perspective, a perspective which was surely still coloured by the vestiges of a mortal, human consciousness which was a long way from fully understanding the enduring machinations, the eternities upon eternities spent witnessing the cycles that transcend the fiercely limited, earthly views of creation and destruction, life and death.

My view, I knew, was still nowhere near my father's view. His perspective was far wider than that of any human, or even angel, and stretched back through the mists of time to the birth of this infernal world.

The portals distilled hope, as well as creating it. The correct use of them could alter the course of events across infinities.

Through the portals, one could travel vast distances in the blink of an eye. These portals, at least those to the lower realms, were immensely difficult to create, and only a demon of my father's power could have pulled off the ability to change the nature of these junctures from their anciently established limitations to open crossroads of free egress.

Yet it seemed that my father was naïve, or had appeared to be, to what must have been a flawed estimation on my part. However my father's plan was blossoming, in that moment he appeared to be struggling against the forces of five part-humans and the annoyances of the lower demonic legions.

It had hardly been a week, I had felt, since I set up the portal at the site of the sixth-century Parisian abbey known as the Célestine, a place of worship rumored to have been used by the Frankish rulers and aristocracy at the time for secret Pagan rituals. Like them, it was Catholic for political expediency only—most had secret Pagan beliefs, and this was one such place for them to practice discreetly.

Additional reasons for choosing that spot were far more pragmatic. The region had an abundant amount of ley-lines converging upon it, and thanks to the rites I had enacted, that was only the beginning.

The fact that the church was long considered cursed and had been razed to make way for a supermarket was just entertaining icing on the cake.

Unlike my hard-earned portals in Rome and Switzerland, I could feel the pride of that portal connecting Paris, the fae realm, and the underworld still standing as I manned the tedious post guarding this bardo-like passage between the lower realm, the fae realm and the Earth side of the Madrid portal. It seemed it was all so my father put on a show for the angel and her little friends.

"You know that it's been collapsed," a tinny voice buzzed from somewhere annoying close to my ear.

"It is?" I asked, my voice sounding too tinged with angst for my own liking as the dragonfly demon buzzed around to face me.

"The team drove us all out," the sickening little thing buzzed at me. "The circle lost its power."

"Quit eavesdropping on my thoughts," I snarled, swatting at the thing while trying to hide my disappointment that yet another piece of work had been destroyed.

"It was your old school chums," the insect demon buzzed as more of his kind started buzzing towards where I stood guard. "And I wasn't eavesdropping. You project your thoughts pretty loudly."

"Bullshit," I snarled.

"It's true," the demon insisted as it landed on my shoulder and crawled down my chest to my waistband where I shoved it away from my crotch to my back. "Quit projecting. It's annoying."

"What are you on about?"

"You're still on about the damn girl."

"What!" I exclaimed before swatting fervently but uselessly as more little creatures started swarming in and out of the small bardo. "You're all mixed up in your tiny brain."

"Shhh," the demon said, crawling back up to my shoulder.

"You're a failure, and I'm tired of listening to it, you human loser. You'll never be a demon."

"I am a demon!" I protested, my voice beginning to rise.

"If you were a demon, you wouldn't be stuck in this bardo with us, scuttling around in the dirt. Ha! If you were a demon, your father would be working for Lucifer, not languishing in the pit of agony he is in right now, thanks to his son's incompetence."

"I'm not incompetent," I protested.

"The only thing Kalgin did right is fool your frail, feeble human mind," a grotty little voice echoed from the far end of the passage as a band of hairy little satyrs came waddling in from nowhere. "The lord of the underworld will make Kalgin pay for his treachery. Your daddy's in hell, little boy."

"No fucking shit, goat boy," I snarled, thoroughly sick of that claustrophobic bardo and the way its transient inhabitants played with my mind the way demons were supposed to play only with human minds.

"Careful," the demon sitting on my shoulder warned. "These are nothing more than lowly beasts of lower minds than the average dog or even cat. They're not worth your time."

"Stop it. I do the gaslighting here, buggy."

"You'll never be a demon."

It became a chant, surrounding me.

"Shit!" I cursed, swatting fruitlessly in every direction.

"Except over millennia," the thing nearest my ear buzzed. "He's got more little spawn than you've got brain cells. What makes you think he gives half a cunt-fart about you, human?"

The thing became more irritating as it joined in the chant with its mates.

"You'll never be a demon. You'll never be a demon. You'll never be a..."

"Just piss off, you lot," I grunted, pushing my way out of the circle of demons.

I wasn't going to let some smelly, greasy little demons with crooked horns get to me. I wasn't. It was just my own fear that was doing this to me.

There was no use in blaming these poor, ugly little bastards who would be poor, ugly little bastards for eternity. With that in mind, I just let their dull yet noisy taunting wash over me, waiting for it to end but knowing that at least it would end, sometime.

At least none of them were crossing over into Earth or the fae kingdom.

Oddly enough, once I surrendered to it, every single one of the little shits chose that moment to scuttle back towards the lower realm. I figured they didn't really feel like being in that cramped little realm any more than me. There was a notion that I just could not shake. Unlike all the other doubts I had been having, I was just too fucking tired to rationalize away the feeling, the knowledge, that those hairy, snarly, buzzy little beasts were correct about one thing: I was being used.

Maybe it was seeing all the hard work I had put into these portals being popped like party balloons, but I could not bear another moment labouring for Kalgin as my dignity dissolved before my eyes. Plus, I knew he could not care less about me. Why should I give a fuck about him?

I stepped away from my tiny post in the bardo and towards the only place where I could get some damned fresh air: the fae realm.

As soon as I could see the shimmering barrier where one world bled into the next, I walked up to it.

From the passage where I stood, there were no epic transformations and feverish visions and confused tumbling as I traveled between realms.

It was as simple as pushing the toe of my loafer into the doorway.

As I did, the barrier shimmered, flexed, and then nearly

burst like a bubble before opening up a small doorway for me to step through.

The other side of the portal was lush and green. The air was great.

I could even see a beautiful castle shining in the sunlight not too far away.

The fae realm…

For a moment, everything seemed perfect. I could see fairies flitting about through the trees and smell the fresh flowers that were everywhere.

And then I noticed the ogre laying face down on a rock nearby, snoring as it blocked the only path to the castle.

It seemed like a place out of the story books I used to secretly covet and take comfort in during my days trying to make a life in London. I was not treated much better there than anywhere, but unlike Earth or the lower realms, the Kingdom of the Fae, which by then seemed more peaceful and quiet, had plenty of open space and places to just…exist.

Walking through the meadow, I was enjoying it already much more than I had during my time at the palace. I realised that the recent history of the place, its destruction, and my role in it were things my human side may have to reckon with. And when that reckoning came, it may have been enough to finally destroy my humanity once and for all. Or, it could potentially destroy everything within me—human and demon alike.

These thoughts were surfacing quickly and uncomfortably as I continued walking in no particular direction, down a path which led through the field of flowers in front of me towards the palace. As I made the decision to turn away from the palace for reasons I could not quite comprehend, everything I was thinking, feeling, considering, my entire thread of egoistic narrative was upheaved and forcefully redirected.

It happened in a heartbeat.

I never even caught sight of my attacker before my

peaceful stroll was brought to an abrupt close with an array of bright green and blue lightning flashes all around me, as well as a powerful blow that felt like a blacksmith's hammer had smashed into my head, followed by a searing pain that ran through my skull and down my spine.

The force was so great, I actually saw stars, and for a moment I thought both my demon and mortal sides had succumbed to the attack and I was indeed as dead as I could be.

I remained on the ground, holding my head and feeling its incessant pounding for what seemed like hours until the pain finally subsided to a dull ache. My usual perception of things returned along with some of my bearings after a moment of reeling from that ridiculously powerful blow.

At first, there was a sudden, powerful realisation that I had not been laying there for hours, but maybe half a minute at most. I had no time to contemplate my return to reality before serving that a massive boot was slowly descending towards my face.

"What's this?" a voice from above moaned. "The second-banana of a half-demon has finally decided to grace us with his presence? What in the almighty *fuck* are you doing here, Zavier?"

I was still recovering when the boot quickly met its target, and I only barely managed to turn my head in time to avoid being hit directly in the face.

The top of my skull felt like it was on the precipice of exploding when it made contact with the giant boot. I grunted loudly, but managed not to shout. Instead, I focused on rolling out of the way before another blow could be landed.

"Don't you ignore me, you little prick!"

The boot that had missed me landed a couple centimetres from my head, sending bits of debris into my face. As much as was still resonating through me, I decided it best not to stick around in that prone position.

Without waiting for another opening, I immediately jumped to my feet, or rather, I attempted to.

There had clearly been some fae magic in the way he had knocked me down at first. Those dazzling electric bolts of light out of nowhere, the sensation of pain which had suddenly surrounded me, followed by a slow-fading confusion. But by that point my attacker had given in to pure, unbridled anger as he stomped around wildly.

That was, until he decided to slam me to the ground once again with a tackle which, to his continued credit, I did not see coming.

Not even close.

"You little shit!" he growled, seething as he held me down on the dirt path. "Did you really think you could show your face here?"

I knew that voice. "Fae boy? I mean, Troy?"

The moment I uttered that name, I felt the weight on top of me start to shift and ease up slightly. "Do not try your tricks with me, Zavier."

My eyes were still struggling to adjust as I stared up at the sky. I heard a few footsteps as the hands let go of my shoulders and arms.

"What are you doing here?" I managed to utter, slowly sitting up and rubbing my head.

"I could ask you the same," he said, standing tall above me. "Are you following me?"

I shot up to a standing position, glaring at him. "No. Why would I follow you?"

Troy, seemingly hesitant, stepped back, his face grim and stoic as ever. He cocked his head to the side, and opened his mouth to speak, but quickly shut it again.

"You're up to something," he said, narrowing his eyes at me.

I extended my hand out to him, so that he could help me up, but withdrew it before he could grab it. "I'm not trusting you enough to help me up."

He huffed, rolling his eyes. "If you're not here to follow me, and you're not here to reign more destruction upon my, I mean, upon *this* kingdom, then why are you here?"

I smirked, my hand slowly moving closer to him. "You'll see soon enough."

Troy grabbed my hand, pulling me up. I kept my balance, resisting the urge to smack him in the face.

What's more, I could not think of a real reason, or even a fake reason, why I was in the fae kingdom.

"You will have to come with me," he said. "There is one thing that I need you for and right now I'll tell you that you had better do it."

"Fine by me," I said, shrugging.

Troy folded his arms, still giving me a cold stare. "I hope you know where my father is."

"So do I," I said under my breath.

With that, Troy took a hold of my arm and led me out of the clearing and through the trees.

"I trust that you know where to go from here," I said, trying to get a sense of direction.

Troy frowned, his grip on my arm tightening. "Shut up and keep quiet."

He led me through the trees for a few minutes, before we arrived at a dirt path. It looked like a road, though it was dirt, not asphalt. It stretched out ahead of us, gently curving to the left down a hill.

"Where is he?" Troy snapped. "I don't know. I know you will give me a hard time, so let's get on with it."

"Oh, I thought you knew," I replied, honestly. "He's in the other palace. You were going in the right direction, actually."

Troy stood there for a good, long moment. A few long

moments, I should say, as his arms uncrossed slightly and his eyes studied mine.

"You're telling the truth, aren't you?"

"You sound surprised," I grinned.

My bearings from my recent time in the realm were returning to me as I was feeling a very curious sense of relief. I did not question why.

"There..." I pointed to the somewhat shorter stone turrets over the horizon, slightly to the left from where we stood to the towers of the main palace. "That is where your pops, the king, is currently, Troy. At least, the last I heard."

The fae boy, and former fae prince, Troy, stood staring silently at the palace in the distance for another long few seconds. At first I was ready to tell him that I was doing him a favor, so let's just get the fuck on with this already. But, as Troy had his poignant little moment staring at where his father dwelt—both his human and fae sides surely playing into the melodramatics going on in his head and heart—I realised that I honestly had nowhere better to be, so I let him have his cornball moment.

"Thank you," he said out of nowhere, staring at the palace.

"Huh?" I furrowed my brows.

"Thank you for doing this for me."

I opened my mouth to tell him where he can stick his fucking thank yous, but I quickly stopped myself. "Come on..." I started venturing off the dirt path. "I know a shortcut."

The fae boy hesitated, looking at me with confusion. "A shortcut? Wouldn't it be easier to just walk along the path?"

I glanced at him with a frown. "My charitability is starting to wear thin."

Without another word, I took off into the woods, ducking under branches and jumping over roots. I did slow down a bit when I heard Troy struggling to follow at my pace.

"How do you know of this shortcut?" he asked.

"It just seemed shorter to go this way," I shrugged,

remaining honest. I laughed silently to myself as I heard Troy grumbling under his breath behind me. When I reached the entrance to the fae king's palace, I stopped.

"Well?" I said, turning.

He'd caught up within seconds, trying his best to hide the maudlin sentiments written clearly all over his face.

"Well, what?" Troy did his best to look and sound commanding and royal or some shit. "Take me to see him." I tried not to laugh too loudly as I pushed open the palace gates.

"Sure thing, Your Highness."

"Your sense of humour is uncanny," he muttered angrily under his breath. I threw my hands up as I strolled inside the palace gates. The palace guards did not even bat an eye as they recognised me and my companion. "It's been like this for a while now. Like I said, your plan was not a bad one at all, Your Highness."

Troy grabbed my arm roughly as soon as we reached the foyer. "And you said that they wouldn't let me in to see my father." It was more of an accusing statement than a question.

"I didn't say that," I replied, my voice low. "I said that I wasn't sure if they'd let you in to see him. There's a difference."

He let go of my arm and crossed his own arms aggressively. "Fine. Let's go see my father."

I bit my tongue to stop myself from saying anything. As much as I wanted to tell him that he was an idiot and that there was no purpose to whatever he thought he was doing there, I decided just to let things play out. We walked through the hallway and approached the great wooden door at the end of the hallway.

I raised my clenched first and rapped my knuckles against the door. I could feel the lump in my throat growing by the second. That was not a usual feeling for me, but this situation was uniquely unpredictable, and that was something I enjoyed, sometimes more than others. What I did know was that Troy's father would be in a rather interesting state.

The door cracked open slightly, and a single eye peered out from the crack. After recognizing me, the door swung open to reveal the fae king.

He looked the same as he did when I last saw him days earlier, when my own father and a few of his closer minions had just finished a little bit of a ceremony, one could call it, with the fae king. Long blond hair pulled back into a ponytail. Clean shaven. Robes of various colors. Pointy ears and bright green eyes. The whole package.

"Zavier, what brings you here?" he said in his soothing voice that I had learned to despise and admire all at once.

I opened my mouth to answer, but Troy pushed me aside and stepped forward.

"We're here to see you," he declared, puffing out his chest and looking his father directly in the eye.

"I figured that much," the fae king replied, not moving a single muscle. "Come in."

He turned and walked farther into his home, leaving the door open for us. The door led directly into the modest throne room.

Troy wasted no time in walking into the palace, but I lingered for a moment.

I looked down at my feet, shaking my head. There was still time to go back. Why was I putting myself through this? It wasn't like any of the work Kalgin asked of me was very difficult—including helping to put a mind control curse on Troy's father. However, I was not currently in control of that, and Troy had no idea his father was under mind control at all. I did not know how he would find out, if he would find out, what would happen. So, I just stood back and watched.

The throne room was very elegant, obviously taken from some sort of French castle. The fae king was sitting in an armchair, not looking at us, as he stared into the fire. When Troy walked in, he stood and stared at Troy, and me behind him.

"Troy...Why are you here?" he asked, and I could hear a ragged bewilderment in his voice already.

"Father..." Troy started, then stopped. He clenched his fists, and continued, as if he was struggling to keep himself from crying. "Father, we need your help."

"Who is 'we'?" the fae king asked loudly. "Is this your entourage, boy?" I stepped around from behind Troy. The fae king looked at me for a moment. Then he got a hostile, rage-laden look in his eyes. "You!" he shouted. "I thought I'd burned you to ash!"

"You did, Your Majesty," I said, calmly.

"Don't you dare call me that!" the fae king shouted furiously.

"Okay," I said. "I would like to talk to you about the portals you made for the demons."

"The portals? What?" he asked, bewildered again. His attention was torn between me and his anger at seeing me.

"Yes, you created the portals," I repeated. The only thing I was sure of with the mind control curse was that the king would be agreeable to a fault and beyond.

"Yes... I did create them," the king stated flatly, his voice empty of all emotion as he stared off into space.

"Stop this, right this minute!" Troy bellowed with an intensity that took even me by surprise. And I hung around with demons.

"What is this?" Troy continued, his emotions starting to come flooding out as his eyes reddened and he struggled to catch his breath.

"Troy," I began.

"You!" Troy took a rather belligerent step in my direction.

"Your father is under a mind control curse."

That did stop Troy in his tracks, but he continued to glare at me, clearly not believing a word I was saying until:

"I am under a mind control curse," the king confirmed, his voice still sounding monotone and detached.

Troy spun around to face his father. "The demons, they only mean us harm."

The fae king shook his head, "No, the demons are our friends, Troy. The humans are the enemy."

As much as it pained me to see this display, I couldn't help but get caught up in the moment as I watched father and son argue about something neither of them were wrong about.

"I always thought I had lost you," Troy said to his father. "But now I am sure of it."

Well, goddamn, I thought. *This fae's over the top emotions are sure infectious sometimes.*

"I can break it," I said to Troy, who immediately spun back around to look at me.

"Why should I believe you?" he asked.

"Because," I explained, looking right in Troy's eyes. "Have I lied to you since you've been here?"

He shook his head. "No, but that doesn't mean you won't start." It was a fair accusation, I figured. Still, I had to convince him of this. "I know of the curse on your father," I said. "The magic is black and rotten, and that's me saying that. No good comes from it, trust me."

"Do it then," he said. "Break it."

"Sure." As I was preparing to do just that, Troy got it in his head that he wanted a bit extra.

"And help me bring him back to Madrid, I can create another portal." Yet again, I was just about ready to go along with my instinct of telling Troy to go fuck himself, but I realized that might not be the most beneficial thing to do .

"Tell you what," I told him, "I'll take you right to the portal I've already set up."

15

THE BIG BANG

Natasha

"You're not doing this," I said to him. "I am."

I no longer had control over my body and was reduced to a spectator. What I was confident in, or at least what I thought I was confident in, was my growing ability to summon the power of pure light to make short work of any demon bastard. The problem was, Kalgin was not just any demon bastard. And after getting those words out, words I meant as a threat, I was completely paralysed once again both inside and out.

"Ah, come on. You're making this too easy for me," he said as I helplessly watched from the corner of my eye as he walked over to me, raising his palm with the movements of someone readying to slap. A slap? I thought to myself. It seemed so tame.

"Don't you dare lay a finger on her." I heard Michael's voice, struggling to make out the words from somewhere behind me, barely able to move, from the sound of it, just as I was.

"Don't you dare lay a finger on either one of them," Kieran's nearly immobile voice chimed in after that. Those daft bastards, was all I could think as I pushed and strained with every fibre of my being to move, to activate, to summon my power or my fists or just fucking something to try and protect my poor, daft, absolutely lovely teammates from the wrath of one of hell's highest demon priests. But it was no use.

I couldn't move. I couldn't do anything. I could only watch as Kalgin stopped in front of my face, before speaking once more.

"No, I don't think I will," he said softly before walking away.

It happened so fast after that. He backhanded Michael first—I could tell by the sound of the demon's hand on his face—sending him flying into the wall I could see in front of me, where he slumped down it, motionless.

Hearing Kalgin's slow, deliberate footsteps behind me, I knew he was walking in Kieran's direction. I trudged, I toiled, I strove and laboured so hard to activate my power or just any part of myself. But I was still hopelessly immobile as the sound of Kalgin's palm slamming against Kieran's face sent an enormous crack echoing through the room. After I heard Kieran's unconscious body drop to the floor behind me, it was silent for what felt like an eternity times infinity until I heard Kalgin's footsteps coming back in my direction.

"You. You're the one who's been getting in my way for the past decades," he said, and I knew very well that he was speaking to me. There was no doubt about that, I could feel it. And then the footsteps stopped, as if he had realised something. "Oh... and you are an angel, aren't you?"

Kalgin's voice changed from that of bitter hatred to one of cruel curiosity. It sent a shiver down my spine, and not a good one.

"No. I'm not." Somehow, I was able to speak again, with some pain and effort.

"Oh? So you're a fallen one, then?"

"I am no such thing," I said, feeling the weight of the entire world in balance, desperate to think of some way out of Kalgin's imminent victory.

Even though we both knew full well what I was.

"Then what are you, exactly? Surely you must be something."

"I am human," I lied, but I could hear the hatred return to his breathing.

The medusa-like grip that Kalgin's pure dark eyes had on me had been growing, and grew again as he drew himself closer to me.

I could feel his face so close to mine that I could almost feel the texture of his rough skin.

"A human? A filthy, disgusting, mortal, miserable human?"

"Yes," I said.

"You lie!" he snarled, just as I knew he would.

I had never felt such fear. So, naturally the next thing I said was, "Fuck you, Kalgin. Do what you want to me, but all you'll ever have is an eternity of being a miserable little shit."

The room was silent once again.

"I have always done whatever I want, mortal," he said. "And I will keep on doing so."

Then, I heard a ripping sound. My heart leaped into my throat, and as the world turned upside down, it fell into my stomach. The world turned pitch black as my eyes were covered by something.

Then, I felt myself falling through the air.

It did not last long, as I soon felt myself back in that strange, large room in Madrid. But it was hot. It was uncomfortable. It was more than that. It got hotter, and the heat was inside of me, scorching the inside of my skin, starting at the bottom of my toes and traveling upwards with a glacial slowness.

My ears started to ring from the pain, and my eyes shut themselves as a reflex.

It got hotter still, even in the parts of me that lay covered, and I heard something bursting. Water? No. Something worse, something like blood gushing out of me. It did not stop. I screamed for it to stop, but it only got hotter still. Something inside me had broken.

"Relax," said that voice, that awful voice of Kalgin's, sounding as if it were in some cave in the distance. "I'm taking your angelhood so you can be a woman at last. A regular, human woman."

The heat continued to burn as the ringing in my ears continued. I felt him cutting something inside of me, and then I felt something coming out of the opening that was my wound. It felt like water, or blood. I couldn't tell which.

"You'll bleed for a few days," said that terrible voice of his. "But then you will be a true mortal. You will live. You will die. And I will be there to make sure you do both."

The heat increased, as did the ringing in my ears.

"The congregation will get you, monster! Your kind is going to die!" I yelled at him.

"We'll see about that," said the voice of Kalgin. "Because the portal is ready."

I felt myself being ripped open wider as something else came out of me. There was a burst of cold air inside of me, and then an explosion of pain. I screamed, and screamed, and screamed.

But there was no sound.

It seemed impossible, but it was clear that my hearing had gone.

The last thing I felt was something pulling me upwards. My body was lifted into the air and then turned upside down as I dangled there. Then, I was pulled in two and the top half of my body was ripped away from the lower half, as if my waist had been sliced open.

While I could not hear, I could feel. I could feel every nuance of agony.

I was sure I was screaming, but, at least for a long moment, I heard nothing.

As my sense of hearing slowly returned, I could make out the shuffling of Kalgin's feet as he scurried away from my dying body and my faltering screams. The last thing I saw was his back as he ran away.

I could feel myself dying.

There was some part of me that had no body. I could sense it. I could feel my entire body, but something fundamental, something that had always been there whether I realized it or could describe it or not, was wasting, burning away fast.

Though my body was burning up, something else within me was cutting down to the bone. Something that could only be described as angelic energy and power was bleeding out of me. My angelic essence, that was what was burning.

It would seem the director had been correct about the nature of angels. That they were indeed made of something, angelic energy or an essence that powered them and gave them their abilities.

The power was there, some auxiliary well of it left, but it was fading, evaporating fast. I could see again, crystal clearly, as Kalgin was growing, inflating almost, his horns stretching and curling, his arms stretching into wings, his legs stretching into a reptilian tail, everything growing fur and scales.

He was evolving, transforming into a higher, stronger, more devilish form. There was a sound almost like air escaping a tire as he grew, a sound even more horrific than Kalgin's own voice.

"Natasha!" I heard my name being called.

Just before I lost all senses, all consciousness, all purpose and meaning in this world, all of it slipping away from me forever, I heard Zavier's voice.

Then, there was nothing.

Then, there was everything.

Then, there was the Big Bang. At least that's what it felt, looked, and sounded like. And then, there was light. Bright, really gosh darn bright white light and a deafening bang. I was much like what I had seen and heard when summoning my own power. Except, instead of the usual feeling of it draining afterwards, I felt power, energy, the blissful spark and spirit of life returning, flowing into me.

They say that you forget your time in the womb, but I didn't. It was all there, every bit of it, clearer than when I had experienced it first hand. Like when you're dreaming and can remember everything about everyone you meet in the dream, even after you wake up.

It was like that, but for the first time, I was experiencing it when I was awake.

That ultimate feeling of anima, of the pure comfort of life, of my life and who I was, continued to wash over me as my eyes opened wide to see Kalgin collapsing, devolving into a wrinkly mess on the ground. Behind him was Troy, and someone who looked like Troy but a bit greener with longer hair, and a whole mess of what looked like fairy-folk, themselves surrounded by that dazzling, brilliant light, and...

"Zavier?" As I spoke that word in confusion, the slithery heap of wrinkles that was Kalgin shot towards me in a flash of a second. The feeling as he grabbed me was indescribable. Not the agonizing pain I'd felt earlier, but the feeling of all my worst, unspoken fears surrounding my being in a tight embrace. That feeling of my life force flowing into me stopped suddenly as Kalgin started flying, wrapped around my body, up towards the ceiling.

"TROY! ZAVIER! ANYBODY ! HELP!" I screamed, praying to whatever god might be listening. But as the walls of the room started shifting and twisting again, my attention was turned once more to what was in front of me. Up close, I could see that Kalgin's skin seemed to be made up of countless tiny runes and symbols. The symbols seemed to be constantly moving and changing, as if they were each their own growing, changing life form.

He opened his mouth once more to speak, and I prepared myself for whatever horrors a demon might do to me. "Kneel, worm." His voice boomed with an unspeakable force. It was deep but also grating, powerful but also screeching...unbearable. My mind was wracked with pain as his very words seem to attack my thoughts, attempting to turn them against me.

"Y-you c-can't kn-know..." I began to say, trying to muster my own strength against his.

The burning started again at the bottom of my feet, but getting ready to travel through my body again. I shut my eyes but that did no good. I felt the fundamental part of myself, whatever it was, draining again. There was no death. There was no way out.

But then, it stopped. The feeling of my deepest terrors hugging me, the burning agony, the vitality draining, it all stopped, replaced by the sensation of falling from the high ceiling. Compared to what I had just been through, it was not that bad.

"Natasha!" I heard Zavier's voice crying out. Soon enough, I was in his arms.

I didn't know how long I laid there for, but I slowly and surely came to. My eyes opened, and I saw the blurry image of Zavier's face. His eyes were red with tears, his mouth was open in an 'o' shape. Slowly, I raised my arm, moving it towards him. He grabbed my hand and moved closer to me, sniffling all the while.

"Natasha," he said in between sniffles. "I thought you were dead."

"Never thought I'd see you cry," were my first words.

"Must be my damned human side at it again," Zavier replied. "Now, come on, we've still got my fucking bastard of a dad to defeat."

Out of focus in my vision, the unmistakable forms of Kieran and Michael were walking slowly in my direction, or at least somewhere in the vicinity.

My teammates, like me, were still reeling but were recovering from the battle's initial blows.

By this time, I had gotten up. While my mind was still dazed and addled from the experience, I knew I had to fight this demon. Even though he didn't love me, I still loved Zavier and didn't want to see him die. Now that I knew how powerful these demons were, I wanted to make sure Zavier survived this as well.

I channeled all my energy into my legs, finding a brand new source in myself.

I sprung up, slamming my fists into the surprised demon's face. He stumbled backwards, hitting the wall and sliding down. I could see in his eyes that he was dazed. But he wasn't out of the fight yet. There was a crowd of fairies directly behind Kalgin. None of the mean folks I had seen recently in Troy's kingdom, or in Zurich, but a much healthier and happier looking bunch. And by happier I mean pissed the hell off. Unfortunately, so did the congress of little satyr and insect demons who began appearing in the portal behind them. A few of the quite battle-ready looking fae were starting to turn their attentions to the monsters behind them.

"He is the one responsible!" the pony-tailed fae who kind of looked like Troy thundered, trying to focus the faes' attention while pointing to Kalgin's half-deflated back. "Attack and show no mercy!"

"Stop them," Kalgin hissed at the demons in a high-pitched whisper with what I only hoped would be the last of his strength. The fairies did as they were told, as did the demons.

The battle had begun.

The demonic creatures were small but vicious things. Both types of beasts emerging behind the fairies had sharp teeth and long tongues to lap up blood, although as my vision continued to focus I noticed some had bizarre looking proboscises that squirmed in a grotesque, wormlike fashion. The fairy-folk were considerably larger than any of the demons, but the demons had the advantage of being behind the fairies and having monstrous appendages to contend with the faes' arrows, hatchets, and fists. And, of course, whatever magic they could muster. I already had a feeling much of their collective power had been used on that blast which had seemed to fell Kalgin. However, that remained to be seen.

The faes were a spectacular sight. They swooped and dodged with such grace that it was almost as if they had years or decades of experience soaring around and fighting in that weird, cavernous room, as opposed to having just wandered in from their own realm. They took advantage of their size by using their massive armoured limbs to shield themselves from most attacks while they picked away at the demonic creatures with their fists and handheld weapons.

The demons were not stupid, however.

I saw one pluck an arrow right out of the air and another caught a hatchet right before it embedded itself into his shoulder. The demons moved so quickly that it seemed as if the weapons were being pushed away by some invisible barrier, although this didn't stop several from dying at the faes' hands.

Inhaling deeply and rallying whatever energy I had to move back into the fight, I took a step forward as the demons latched onto two faes and viciously attacked them with tentacles that appeared from their mouths and noses.

In the thick of the melee, a tall man in dark corduroy joined the action in a blur. It happened so swiftly that all I saw was his muscular back straining against his reddish-black jacket as he ran towards the demons. It took me a moment to recognise who it was.

"Alexander!"

Alexander quickly pivoted on the balls of his feet to face me for the briefest moment.

"I made it just in time," he uttered quickly in a low voice before continuing to rush forward and join the battle. Witnessing this was an instant jolt of inspiration, hastening the regrowth of my drive and vigour.

Like some errant sneeze, a narrow beam of angelic power escaped from me with only minimal conscious awareness on my part. The moment I had the strength, the thin streak of light struck the middle of the demonic horde with precision, sending the small creatures flying, or fleeing, back into the portal from whence they came.

Even Alexander took a step back as the cloud of monsters were shot in the other direction, away from this realm.

It was as if both the small hairy monsters and the creepy-crawlies were being drained in a blur of brown and black from the earthly realm back into the portal as the fairy-folk turned their focus towards making sure every last one of the horrid things went into the portal post haste.

Unfortunately, as almost everyone present drew their attention to the lesser demons and ensuring their departure, Kalgin was using the reserves of strength he had remaining, and the strength he then had growing, to focus straight on me.

As I took another step in Kalgin's direction, the fairies beat me to the punch.

Literally.

The first few went straight for the kill, shooting arrows and flashing bolts of lightning into Kalgin's eyes. He fell to the floor wailing in agony, trying to pull out the arrows. The rest just started stabbing him repeatedly, like a bunch of vengeful children throwing tantrums.

"Damn, thought they would last longer," Zavier said with a grin.

Alexander shot Zavier an understandably suspicious look and then addressed me. "Do your thing, Natasha."

Feeling a fresh well of life-defining energy like I never had before, I shot a bright blue streak of pure angelic fucking power into the centre of Kalgin's forehead with such precision that the fairies still kicking and stabbing at him barely even noticed. Kalgin let out such a pathetic little screech that I actually started giggling.

"There," I said, feeling proud of myself. "That should hold him." Then, in a moment of clarity, I remembered that me and Zavier were on opposite sides. Zavier was looking at me with a mixture of grudging respect and arousal. "Zavier, what are you doing here?"

"Saving your ass, apparently," he responded with a wink. I couldn't tell if he was being serious or sarcastic. "He's not dead yet! He needs to be drained of his demonic mana, which I can take care of now."

Zavier knelt down next to the still-writhing demon priest, who had deflated further into a pile of reddish grey mangled wrinkles. He was moving, though, there was life still in him indeed. There was near dead silence in the room as we all watched apprehensively. Zavier placed his hand on Kalgin's head, and began speaking to his demon father.

"I am your son, and you are my father. You gave me my powers, to do with as I please. It is your time to sleep, and never wake from that sleep."

There was a gaseous, rancid stink, like sulphur and stale rubber, and Kalgin released some weak words into the air:

"You are my son, you could have had everything." The massive room grew thick with that rotten, rubbery stench as

Kalgin's words became laboured and halting. "It's not. Too. Late."

"I doubt that," Zavier told his father. "And I was just a tool for you, regardless. I do not take kindly to being a tool in anyone's little schemes. You should have realised that those little demons have such big mouths."

Zavier stood, clenched his fist and drove it straight into the shriveled, squirming husk of his father's form. There was a horrid cracking sound as Zavier crushed something buried within those dying demon wrinkles on the ground. That crackling, crunching racket was followed by a sudden, deafening hiss, like air escaping. The room smelled like burnt flesh and smoke mixed with that rotten rubber.

As Zavier continued to crush his father's demon heart—or whatever he was doing to whatever it was—Kalgin let out a pained howl that continued to echo off the walls for a few long seconds even after the demon was silent forever.

"Thanks for my wasted time, asshole," Zavier spat as he removed his fist. The hole he'd left in Kalgin's dead body continued to leak a thick, noxious, hissy cloud.

With a wave of Zavier's outstretched palms, Kalgin's body fell into the portal with a thud, all the stinky clouds surrounding it followed the body automatically, hissing violently. It only took a second or two, and the portal snapped shut as if it had never been there in the first place.

The room was left in a dead silence. At least it was for a lengthy moment as all of the creatures present adjusted themselves from the intensity of the world-saving battle to the new, much more peaceful reality we were suddenly living.

Zavier stood alone, staring at where the portal had once stood, as everybody else in the room began to mill about, checking in on their friends and compatriots and speaking to each other awkwardly as if the whole thing had suddenly become some office cocktail party.

I turned to where Troy was standing with his fellow fae, the one who sort of resembled him but I had never seen previously.

"Can you get my people and I back home?" The Troy-looking fae asked Troy.

"Yes, I can get us back home, Dad." Ah, that made sense.

"I have missed you. The Kingdom of the Fae has missed you, whether you realise that or not. The royal court has been incomplete for eons in your absence."

Troy looked over at me. I tried my best to maintain a neutral expression. We needed Troy on the team for the congregation, but it was not my place to influence him one way or the other when it came to his father's remarkable invitation.

Troy's eyes softened and widened noticeably as he kept looking in my direction. He was, quite clearly, bloody chuffed to be offered a return to his place as prince in his old kingdom.

I tried my best to feel excited for him, and hide how crushed I felt that he could be leaving us.

By then Kieran, Alexander, and Michael had gathered around us as well, and had become absorbed in listening to the conversation. They were standing behind Troy, and by the looks on their faces their feelings were as mixed as mine.

"I am honored, my father," said Troy. "But I cannot, I am more needed here."

"Oh, thank God!" I shrieked out loud. Fortunately, even the king laughed.

"While my heart breaks at your choice, my son, I will not even question it."

"I will answer anyway," Troy responded, looking at me still. "There's someone I need to be here for, in the human realm."

"Will you accompany me on a visit back to the royal palace?" The king asked his son.

"I would be honored," Troy turned back to his father. "My home may be here with the humans, but you will be seeing a lot of me, if you'll have me that is."

"We would be honoured."

"Oh, and you dropped this," Troy handed his father a worn yet gorgeous jewel-encrusted crown. "King."

The king accepted his crown. "Thank you kindly. I will never be able to express how proud I am of you, Prince Troy."

Father and son, king and prince, embraced.

Troy then turned to me. "Natasha, I can transport you and your team back home as well," he said. "Will you come with me?"

I didn't even need to think about it. I just nodded, because I may have been, just maybe, close enough to bursting into tears that saying a single word may have done it.

"Travel safe, everyone." Every single creature in that room, including all the fairies, turned to look at Zavier standing awkwardly by where the portal had been.

"What? What'd I say?"

EPILOGUE: LA PALAIS

Natasha

There may have been a cough or two during the minute or so of silence following Zavier's question.

Finally, Michael let out a couple of heart laughs.

"You know what," Michael said, breaking the silence. "I never thought I'd say this about such an evil bastard, but this Zavier guy is alright."

The silence was broken as there were a couple of small, stray laughs then everyone stared milling about the room and talking, shaking off some of the pent-up energy from the battle.

Kieran looked around the large space as he approached Prince Troy and me.

"What is this place again?" he asked. "I know I found it, but..."

"Madrid," I answered.

Apart from Troy, I didn't think I'd ever heard a fae laugh

before. Mostly, I'd just seen them act angry. However, as the King of the Fae laughed at my joke, it was like the ringing of deep, lush, sonorous bells.

"I like you, Natasha."

It was, in a way, a mild-mannered compliment. The king was certainly a seasoned diplomat, though, the way he had figured out my name during the height of all that insanity and used it when addressing me.

And, I was already feeling emotional to begin with, so I simply smiled and nodded. Because you know what they say:

Every time a fairy laughs, Natasha cries.

Happy tears.

"I know what this building is, actually." Zavier approached us, about as shy as I had ever seen him. "Metro de Madrid Headquarters," Zavier smiled lightly.

"Why did you and your father choose this for your portal then?" Kieran sneered.

"There is a transit strike," Zavier replied, not really explaining. "So it wasn't going to work anyway."

"I am sure there were reasons," I said softly. "But it doesn't have to matter now."

"What?" Zavier seemed confused.

Also, the rest of them were staring at me like I had three heads.

"Zavier," I asked him, "why are you still here?"

"Um... Is that a trick question?" he asked me in return. "Because we won?"

"But why are you still here, specifically?"

He was silent for a moment.

"I don't know," Zavier admitted. "It never occurred to me to leave. Does it matter? I'm not my father."

"Of course," I told him. "I'm sorry, I just..."

"It is over," said Zavier. "I saw that, I don't want it. Humanity won."

"No," I said. "It's not over. That was just one demon, and a portal. There are more. There will always be more, it seems."

I had always sensed some hidden sadness in Zavier, and I sensed it even now.

He had started out this whole recent odyssey to help himself, and he ended up helping nobody but, well, everybody. We had witnessed him close the portal and put the last rather hefty nail in the coffin of Kalgin's plans. He saved the world with nothing in it for himself, and he knew that only he was to blame for still being met with scorn and distrust.

"Zavier, we need competent people." As I listened to my own words leave my mouth, a bit shocked at what I was saying, Alexander appeared beside me and immediately echoed the sentiment that I wanted to shout at myself:

"Are you mad, woman? What are you saying?"

Zavier just looked towards the ground and chuckled quietly at Alexander's yelling. For once, I was not sure what Zavier was thinking. Yet I could tell he was uncomfortable, which was also a first.

"Wait, this isn't happening." Kieran seemed to have suddenly started to realize what I was implying. "Natasha, you know what he has done to us, and you."

"He cannot be trusted," Michael added, his voice as even, calm, and brimming with uneasiness as I had ever heard it.

"I'll be on my way, then," Zavier said, seeming to have little to no interest in the odd drama I had started.

Yet everyone's objections, even Zavier's, were having the strange effect of making me feel more sure in my decision to, well, welcome Zavier aboard to the side of good.

"The past is the past." I shrugged. "We need to move forward, and with his background, Zavier could be an invaluable asset. He can help us close that last portal, for one."

I noticed Zavier, despite his words, had not made any moves to leave.

He had nowhere to go, after all.

"You know how I trust your decisions, Natasha, and even your intuition. But this..." Alexander pointed in Zavier's direction. "This idea may very well be beyond my ability to stomach."

"We'll be able to call upon the help of a demon any time we need it," I said. "Just think about that."

There was a pause in the conversation, an almost surprising silence considering how high passions seemed to be running.

It seemed possible that my teammates were actually considering this.

"I have to say, I'm still unsure. What if this is a trick?" Michael said.

Zavier stood there, not speaking a word.

"It's a risk, but I trust Zavier," I responded. "Because I have—all of us have—been granted trust, in good faith, when we needed it most."

"None of us have done what he has!" Kieran shouted.

"He's right," agreed Zavier. "While I want no part of my late father's world any longer, I could not ask to be accepted into the congregation now."

"Do you want to be?" I questioned him point blank.

Zavier went from looking vaguely in our direction to gazing back down on the unfinished flooring. I knew that if he wanted to say no, he would have said that immediately.

I could feel the change in tone at the lack of an immediate denial from Zavier. It was as good as him admitting to us that, yes, he was actually considering this.

And that was enough to give me a bit of a scare and consider what it was offering a little more.

We all knew what Zavier was capable of, but I had long had a special feel for it. There was something in the way he thought I had always been able to grasp—intuitively, as Alexander had implied.

Thanks to that intuition, I knew that despite his selfishness and callous personality, he was reliable when it came to putting his mind on something, on focusing and taking whatever larger task at hand there was with dead seriousness.

"If Zavier joins, he is on our side," Michael said, again breaking the silence. "I hope he realises that," he continued, staring straight at Zavier.

Also thanks to my intuition, I knew that Zavier was in that place where all of us had been, that place where he needed acceptance the most.

"I realise that, of course," Zavier replied to Michael's statement. "And if I join, I accept that. It's what I wanted long before any of this other nonsense."

"Do as you wish," Alexander scowled, seeing where the sentiment was heading and not liking it in the least.

I looked to Kieran and Michael after Alexander stormed off.

Michael was just looking down—strangely enough in the same way that Zavier had been throughout much of the conversation. It was a relief to hear Michael laugh softly to himself, even if it was only laughter at the tension.

"You seem really weirdly determined, Natasha," Zavier said, finally speaking. "But I don't think I can do that."

Zavier offered no reasoning for his refusal, but of course he did not owe me any.

Resigned, I shook my head.

"That's fine," I told him. "You have no obligation to the congregation or anybody. Just, if you ever need anything, please call on us."

"Will do," he nodded, looking at me.

I turned from him and started towards where Troy and his father were talking and laughing, thinking about the journey home ahead of us. I spotted Alexander speaking with them as well. It was pleasant to see that he had not gone off to brood alone.

"Natasha," Zavier called. I turned to him again, as did the rest of the team. "Thank you."

"It was nothing," I told him. "Just part of the job."

He nodded. "I want...do you really want me to be part of it?"

Alexander, immediately upon hearing those words, had run off to sulk again somewhere. I looked at Troy and Kieran.

They had both taken to staring at the floor again, which seemed to go into fashion the moment I suggested this whole crazy idea.

Michael refused to look up, he just shrugged slightly and let out another small, uncomfortable laugh.

Kieran, however, looked up from his shoes to glare directly at Zavier.

"That's up to him," said Kieran. "But either way, Zavier, just make sure to close up that last fuckin' portal, would ya?"

That was not what anyone of us expected Kieran to say.

"In La Palais," Zavier said, still looking down. "Consider it done."

"Good." With that, Kieran started walking towards the door.

Good, I thought.

That's what I wanted to believe in.

To be continued…

NEXT IN THE SERIES: MORTAL
DESIRES

I must outsmart the human hunters or I'll end up as their experiment.

With humans discovering the existence of Creatures, we're no longer safe. When werewolf pups are kidnapped, my team decides that enough is enough. I'm certain that our combined abilities—my angelic power, Keiran's werewolf strength, Alexander's vampire speed, Troy's fae shrewdness, and Michael's shifter skills, will lead us to success.

Yet instead of rescuing the pups, we fall straight into a trap. I wake up in a high-tech cell, separated from my friends, surrounded by scientists eager to study me. Through sheer determination, I manage to find Kieran and escape. Unable to locate the others and too weak to fight, we flee to lick our wounds.

Keiran nurses me back to strength. His warm body keeps me protected from the cold. Soon, the feelings between us heat up. I can't resist sweet, loyal Keiran even though I still care for Troy and Alexander. Is it possible to love three men? Can it end well?

I don't know and there's no time to ponder my love life. Keiran and I need to return to the research fortress to get our friends.

Will we succeed, or will we end up in a cell?

Mortal Desires is the third book in The Angel's Guardians series. The book ends in a cliffhanger. Don't miss this delicious paranormal reverse harem romance filled with magic, sizzling romance, and heart-pounding action!

Coming in April 2021!

Sign up for Callie's Newsletter now so you can be the first to hear about her new release:
https://dl.bookfunnel.com/ovzzd2h3t1

Thank you so much for reading Demonic Affairs, and I hope you enjoyed this adventure. I had a lot of fun writing it!

In the next book, Mortal Desires, even though Natasha and her team have managed to banish Kalgin back to Hell, all is not peaceful. Humans are now very aware of the existence of Creatures.

Everything is falling apart and the lives of every living Creature is in danger. And the biggest prize of all that everyone wants to get their hands on is Natasha, the angel. Everybody wants a piece of her. Literally.

Will things ever return back to the way they were? Or will the Creatures have no choice but to turn tail and hide for the rest of millenia?

I hope you enjoyed it. If you have a moment, please write a short review for it. As an indie author, this means so much to me when it comes to my books reaching more readers. I personally read all of your reviews, and they give me so much motivation to keep writing. Even a sentence or two helps!

>>CLICK HERE TO WRITE A REVIEW<<

PS. I'll also be so happy if you'd like to stay in touch for my new release, discounts, giveaways and fun stuff!

You can also get a copy of the story about Director Emilio and his lifetime lover. You don't want to miss it!

Get the prequel for this series completely for FREE here: https://dl.bookfunnel.com/ovzzd2h3t1

Love,
Callie

ABOUT THE AUTHOR

Callie Stone is an avid writer and her writings give a new vibe to the fantasy and paranormal romance genre.

In high school, she met her hero in a friend who introduced her to the world of the paranormal romance novel, and ever since she has carved a niche for herself in the writing world. She has a knack for merging real history and culture with the fantasy world of imagination and serves the mix in her delightful and enchanting paranormal novels.

What she enjoys most is collecting her thoughts by a window seat with her favorite hot chocolate.

Her books bring readers to a new world of imagination with shifters, magic, and thrills. When she is not engaging with her fans, hiking, or enjoying the ambiance of mother nature, Callie spends time in the company of her lovely children and ever-supportive husband as well as her gorgeous cat at her home in Chicago USA.

Ps. You can follow Callie Stone through her newsletter for her latest updates including freebies, sales info, and every new release! And you'll get several recommendations for steamy fantasy books.

Subscribe here: https://dl.bookfunnel.com/ovzzd2h3t1